"What are you afraid of?"

"I don't know," she said, frowning. "I'm afraid of the way you make me feel. It all seems new to me, as if we're on the brink of discovery."

"But we are," he said, the corner of his mouth curving in a smile as the back of his hand brushed her cheek. "You're not like anyone I've ever met before, so there are no guidelines on how we're supposed to act."

Tara steadied herself against him. "But what happens next? What about tomorrow?"

Some men would have promised her everlasting devotion. Others would have given her words to build upon with hope. He could have mentioned love, but he didn't.

"I don't know," he answered. "Can you tell me?"

She shook her head, biting her lower lip. Now was the time to escape . . . if she was going to.

ABOUT THE AUTHOR

Carolyn Thornton is no armchair traveler. In her work as a free-lance travel writer she has visited all over the world, from Costa Rica to Germany to Hong Kong. She has even taken flying lessons in an attempt to transport herself to the exotic locations she loves. It was from her ground-school instructor that she got the idea for the hitchhiking contest in *A Class Above*. When she's not traveling, Carolyn makes her home in Hattiesburg, Mississippi.

A Class Above

CAROLYN THORNTON

Harlequin Books

TORONTO • NEW YORK • LONDON
AMSTERDAM • PARIS • SYDNEY • HAMBURG
STOCKHOLM • ATHENS • TOKYO • MILAN

Published March 1986

First printing January 1986

ISBN 0-373-16144-1

Printed in Canada

Prologue

Dick Shaw challenged Tara Jefferson at the end-of-semester party. When he issued the dare, they were standing next to a table where a bowl of guacamole dip shared space with a newly potted plant. Both were within tempting reach of Tara's hands.

Mentally, Tara sized up the rim of the guacamole bowl and estimated the diameter of the pot containing the plant. She had a hard time deciding which of the two contents would best complement Dick's irritating hair color. Everything about the man rubbed her the wrong way. At first Tara had felt guilty about her dislike of Dick. The better she got to know him, the more she realized everyone in the doctoral program felt the same way.

"Let's investigate risk-taking limits," he said, dipping a potato chip into the guacamole as he talked to Tara.

Yes, green is definitely his color, Tara thought. She watched him pop the potato chip into his smug mouth. The green of envy would be most becoming to his know-it-all eyes. Dragging her mind from a vivid image of guacamole oozing down his face, she listened more intently while pretending increasing disinterest.

"From what I know of you, just from those brief appearances you make at classes—" He paused, looking for a sign that he had irritated her. "I'd say you're the type who doesn't run from a challenge," Dick assessed.

"You've got that right," she admitted. Tara knew that he had spread false rumors among the younger students, saying she didn't mingle at their parties because they were beneath her in experience. The truth was that Tara wanted to be accepted into their group, but redeveloping study habits after years away from school hadn't been easy. She had spent every extra hour with her nose buried in books.

"Have you ever taken any *real* risks?" Dick asked, munching on the chip as he talked.

Tara tried not to laugh. "Plenty of them." From childhood she had always been the first one to act on a dare. Memories flashed through her mind of the forbidden trees she had climbed and the neighbor's bull she had ridden, at the expense of a broken wrist. She had even been the first of her peers to take the greatest risk of all—marriage, resulting in shattered dreams. More recently, leaving her successful counseling practice to go back to school for a doctorate degree had involved a high risk, particularly since she was ten years older than most of the other students in the program. She wouldn't know how that would pay off until after she got her degree and finished her internship. Life-changing decisions involved risk, just like love and marriage.

She looked down at what she had chosen to wear that evening: harem pants to accent her shapely curves and an iridescent headband to highlight her reddish-blond hair. She had selected something youthful and chic to make the other students see that she was trying to fit in with them. Everyone else wore comfortable jeans and casual dresses; but no one had been surprised when Tara stepped out of her car as if she were alighting from the sultan's prize camel. Dick was going to have to learn the hard way that Tara Jefferson was not one to play games with, not if he wanted to win.

"Risk," she said, smiling serenely, "is practically my middle name."

"I thought it would be," he said in a manner that implied a put-down. "What plans do you have over the semester break?" He reached for another potato chip.

Tara was inclined to lurch into him—accidentally, of course—at a crucial moment to send his crisp white shirt sleeve deep into the guacamole. She stiffened to restrain herself. "I don't have any plans," she said, "which is a plan in itself. I don't want to do anything that reminds me of books for the next two weeks."

"What would you say about doing a mini-study over the break involving travel?"

"Do I have to read anything?"

"No."

"Does it involve any writing?"

"No."

"Would this 'study' mean doing something with you?" Next to going someplace with Dick, the only worse thing she could think of was camping. And the only reason she hated that was because it didn't come with room service.

"No," he said, smiling self-assuredly. "I was thinking more in terms of against me rather than with me."

Her mouth curved into a grin. "Go on."

"Let's apply the utility principle to this travel study and make a cost-benefit analysis of hitchhiking."

"Hitchhiking?" she said. "Isn't that a rather elemental subject for a psychological study?"

"Not at all," he defended. "Can you think of a better way to meet people?"

"How about a cruise?" she suggested.

Someone nearby snickered. Tara noticed that their discussion had attracted the attention of half the room, as Dick had probably intended. Throughout the semester he had tried to coax her into competing with him. She had refused because her studies were more important and more taxing than his game playing. Now that they wouldn't be in school for the next few weeks, she didn't have that as an excuse to back away from his challenge. And he knew it. The audience of his peers made it even more difficult for her to refuse. She was sure that he had intentionally saved the question for the party.

"A cruise is too superficial," Dick said hastily. "Hitchhiking gives you a real feel for the grass roots of a place and its people."

"It does seem like your style," she said. Dick was the type who scrounged through the garbage cans rather than pay a dollar for a Sunday paper. He would spend all his life studying and still never learn anything. Some people just needed the books to make them appear intelligent. Others could get by on talent and personality. Dick wasn't one of those. "If it's going to be a travel study," she said, "does it have to be via hitchhiking?"

"Why not? One of us may even be able to turn the adventure into a dissertation."

"You're welcome to use it," Tara said. "I already have my subject approved, thank you."

Realizing the other students were listening intently, Dick detailed the challenge. "Hitchhiking wouldn't take any money," he said, staring at Tara, "and most of us aren't wallowing in dough."

Tara rolled her eyes. It was useless to explain her finances to him. Because she had been in practice, she had built up a fund for her education and the sale of a condo had added to it. But she was far from being a millionaire, as Dick wanted everyone to think. Hattiesburg, the site of the University of Southern Mississippi, wasn't as expensive as her old home in Boston, but it still cost money to live, particularly when she would have no income until after she got her degree. "Wouldn't you have the advantage since there's a higher risk for a woman who's hitchhiking than there is for a man?"

"Slightly," he agreed. "But since you're a female, you would be more likely to get rides."

Her eyebrows twitched upward. If he shaved his beard, he might have some success in convincing strangers he was a halfway decent risk as a rider.

"Besides," he continued, "you're also older, which is to your advantage."

Tara forced a grin to remain on her face as he needled her about her age. "How does age give me the advantage?"

"Maturity and a better sense of judgment are supposed to go with age."

"The same way warm milk and pablum do, I suppose?"

Laughter erupted nearby, but Tara noticed her petite roommate, Julie, frowning beside her.

"That's not what I meant at all," Dick said, trying to defuse his remark. But he flamed her anger as he added, "If we didn't know you're ten years older than the rest of us, we'd think you were younger."

"It's a little more than ten years," she said distinctly, not caring who knew she had just hit the down side of her thirties. It was becoming evident that this contest was a battle of sexes, wisdom against youth and Dick versus Tara.

Someone turned down the stereo. Out of the corner of her eye, Tara could see the students milling into factions. The greater number of classmates were siding with Tara.

"Suppose we take a week of the break and see who can travel the farthest distance solely by hitchhiking?" Dick proposed. He reached for another blob of guacamole as if he had just thought of the rules of the game.

"Isn't this a little childish, Dick?" Julie asked, suddenly making sense of the rumors she had heard the other students discussing. She touched Tara's hand, wishing she could do something to hold her back.

"You only go around once," Dick recited. "Besides, most of us *students* spend the entire summer hitchhiking, backpacking, seeing this country of ours. I'm only suggesting one week."

"Trains and boats and planes are just as effective a means of travel," Tara argued. "I always feel at home where my American Express card is welcomed."

"If you have the money to travel that way," he said, as if it were a crime for Tara to have an established credit rating.

For a long while Tara didn't answer. She wanted to show Dick that she could move up or down the scale to anyone's level, including his. If she played his game, by the time she finished, she wanted him to know once and for all that it only took the intelligence in her little finger to beat him. "How would we prove where we've been?"

"We'll send postcards back here," he suggested. "The postmarks will be dated proof of where we've been. You could write to, umm, Julie here, for instance. I could write to Jim."

Jim moved closer into the group, now that he was included in this battle of wits. Tara glanced at Jim and his wife, who was rocking their newborn in her arms. If Jim were a country, Tara thought, he would be Switzerland. He always took the middle ground to keep peace. Whenever he took an opposing viewpoint, it was because no one else would, and he did so merely for the sake of balance rather than conviction.

Tara looked at Julie, whose frown had deepened as if to say, "Don't let him rook you into this." She tried to ignore the uneasiness that crept over her from Julie's silent messages. "Tara—" Julie began.

Tara interrupted her, speaking on impulse. "Let's make it two weeks, Dick. One week would just be a warm-up."

Chapter One

In spite of the air conditioning, Tara's palms were sweating. She kept fingering the strap of her lightweight flight bag as if staking a claim to it, although she was the only one sitting in the waiting room.

Relax, she lectured herself as if she were one of her patients. *You should be congratulating yourself for your successful first hitchhiking ride. Deal with the anxieties of the next step after you know what you're up against.*

She scanned the clear blue skies again, knowing the next ride was crucial to her plan but trickier to get. It was a good thing Dick had given her so little time to consider carefully the risks and realize how ridiculous this adventure was, she decided. Here she was acting like a frisky college kid on break. And, age aside, she had to remember she *was* a college kid again. That was one of the reasons she had accepted this stupid dare. She wanted to earn the other students' approval, and acting like them seemed a way to fit in. The other reason was that men like Dick reminded her of her ex-husband, Rick. In spite of the number of years since the divorce, Dick's know-it-all attitude and subtle putdowns aggravated old wounds. The challenge to beat

Dick was like an opportunity to prove, once and for all, that Rick's taunts that she would never be able to succeed on her own were unfounded.

Before Tara had gotten home from the party, she had been ready to change her mind. By then Julie had filled her in on details Tara hadn't been aware of. The other students had known Dick planned to challenge Tara at the party, and they had made bets on the outcome. Tara knew how tight student budgets were. She also knew how this group bet on anything to break up the monotonous days of study. Most had lost money because she had said yes to the challenge, which pointed out how little they knew her.

During the term, while the students socialized together, Tara had stayed home or gone to the library to study. After being away from the books for more than ten years, adjusting to a study routine hadn't been easy. She kept remembering what a breeze school had been for Rick, while she had worked so hard for both of them while trying to get an education herself. It had put too much strain on the marriage. Looking back, she realized how her ambitions had threatened Rick, who wanted nothing more than a housekeeper to come home to. By continually putting her down and belittling her accomplishments, he had thought he could keep her under his thumb so that he would always feel more important. Now her bookworm attitude made her appear antisocial, thanks to added comments from Dick to that effect.

"I just knew he was dreaming up something," Julie had said on the drive home after the party. "He's been whistling in the halls for the last two weeks. No sane psychology student is ever happy during exam week. Until you moved into town, he was king of the

campus with grades." She had paused and added, "By
the way, the other kids were glad you topped Dick in
that. A few of them didn't even mind the money they
lost."

"They bet on that, too?" Tara had rolled her eyes
and felt as if she couldn't back out with all of the other
kids' hopes and money riding on her.

But now, as she sat in the small waiting room
watching the skies, the fatigue of the day caught up
with her. Tara couldn't get Julie's warnings out of her
mind.

"Tara, no one will think badly of you if you back
out. It's a childish dare, anyway, and it could be dangerous. You never know who's going to pick you up
or what their intentions might be. Before the week is
over, you could be murdered or run over or worse."
Julie had shivered and pleaded, "Tara, don't do this."

Now, Tara thought, it *could* be dangerous. She was
continually at risk with the people who picked her up.
But so far she had been extremely lucky. Earlier that
morning Jim and Julie had ridden with Tara and Dick
to the starting point of the hitchhiking venture. The
four of them had been jammed into Jim's Volkswa-
gen along with Dick's heavy backpacking gear and
Tara's lighter flight bag. Tara had tried not to giggle
as she thought how appropriate the backpack was for
Dick. Before the two weeks were up, she suspected he
would be doing much more hiking than hitching. If
her plan worked, she would get twice as far in half the
time.

Years of traveling had taught her to pack a minimum of essentials: two pairs of jeans, three blouses,
one sweater and a jacket, a dress, a change of under-
wear, a long T-shirt to sleep in, a pair of heavy wool

socks, in case she got into the mountains or as far north as Canada, a folding umbrella and a minimum of makeup—which was what always took up most of the weight and space whenever she packed. She couldn't exist without her makeup cream to hide the freckles. That morning she had worn her most comfortable shoes, jeans and a blouse. In the button-down pockets of her clothing she carried travelers' checks, her favorite charge card and her passport. She had secured her hair on top of her head in an elegant French braid that made her sculptured cheekbones more prominent. Anyone looking at her would have thought she had just stepped out of a Mercedes that had run out of gas.

Dick, on the other hand, had not bothered to shave. He looked like an escapee from Parchman prison. The only thing that he had neglected to coordinate with his faded jeans and blue work shirt was a ball and chain. He had laughed at Tara's fresh-from-the-shower appearance, telling her she should have dressed more for comfort, as he had. Tara had smiled and said that if she had to ride in a truck with a bunch of cows, there was no reason she had to look like one of them.

"This is the place," Jim had said, pulling the VW onto the shoulder of the road in a bumpy, jolting stop. There had been nothing in sight but pine trees and scrub brush. It had been early, but the sun was already sending heat waves shimmering up from the two-lane highway.

"Good enough for me," Tara had said, sliding out of the car. They were just north of Hattiesburg on old Highway 11. She glanced up the road and could barely see the blinking light on top of the TV tower about a mile or two away. A turkey buzzard circled around a dead animal on the road ahead.

"Fine with me, too," Dick said. His bulky backpack got stuck as he tried to wedge it through the open doorway of the tiny car.

"We'll be waiting for your postcards," Julie called, getting out of the backseat to climb up front with Jim. She gave her roommate a quick hug and whispered, "Please be careful." Then, climbing into the car, she cheered, "May the best hitchhiker win!" Julie hung her head out the window and waved jauntily as Jim put the car into gear and it chugged out of sight.

Watching them drive away, Tara wished she could be more cheerful. She took a deep breath and looked up and down the empty two-lane highway. This really was a silly, risky idea she had agreed to, but she wasn't about to let Dick know how she felt. She clutched her bag to her chest and started to cross the road.

"Where are you going?" Dick demanded. He had barely taken two steps after he had lugged his heavy backpack out of the car and was sitting on top of the pack as if waiting for a magic carpet to float past and sweep him away.

"How should I know?" Tara retorted. "I haven't gotten my first ride yet." She looked up and down the empty highway again and continued to cross the road.

"No, I mean, where do you think you're going right now? Planning to walk all the way for the next two weeks?" he jeered.

Her smile said she hoped nothing but snails passed his way. "I'm not opposed to doing a little walking. It does keep me in shape, considering my age. But all I'm planning to do is cross the road. You wouldn't want anyone to get the wrong impression that we're together, would you?"

"You're right," he said, standing up, hauling his backpack onto his shoulders. "I'll cross the road. You can take this side." He struggled with his heavy backpack. "I don't like the idea of you heading straight back to Hattiesburg. I'm not sure I trust you." He dumped his sack on the other side of the road.

"Don't trust me!" She screeched. "You were the one who dreamed up this idiotic game. How could I possibly cheat by going through Hattiesburg? Do you think you're getting a bigger share of the country to hitchhike in, since this way," she said, thumbing north, "is only three states away from the East Coast?"

He shook his head as if what she was saying wouldn't make sense to a two-year-old. "How am I to know that you haven't arranged with someone to drive you anywhere you want to go? All you have to do is link up with them in Hattiesburg."

"Oh? So that's your game, is it, Dick?" *Damn the man,* she thought. *But even if he has planned to do that, I'm going to beat him!*

"I haven't done that at all," he denied, looking smug. Tara realized then that he had some secret plan. She only hoped it wasn't the same one she had thought of. "I'm merely covering all of the bases."

She tried not to let her uneasiness show. He was probably bluffing, she told herself, to put her at a psychological disadvantage right at the start. Refusing to be intimidated by one of his intellectual mind games, she said, "Fine." She threw up her hands, knowing that it was useless to argue with a lunatic. "Then I'll take this side. Did you even know that if you stay on Highway 11, you can reach Washington or New York?''

"Ha! You'll be doing good to get to the Alabama state line. Women don't know anything about hitch-hiking."

"Is that what this is all about?" she asked, "Male against female? You just watch my dust!" She shifted her bag in her arms and stalked up the highway heading north. The road curved nearly a mile past the point where they had both been dropped. She looked back and saw Dick still sitting where she had left him. Several cars had passed heading his way, but none had stopped for him. The turkey buzzard had shifted its attention from the dead animal to Dick.

After walking about two miles, some of Tara's anger had dissipated. The beginning of a blister had formed on her heel. As each step carried her farther from civilization, Julie's warnings echoed in her mind. "It's too risky... too risky... risky."

After walking another half mile, Tara had a rock in her shoe to add to the blister on her foot. She set her bag down in a patch of red clover and hopped on one foot until she removed the offender. The back of her neck was steaming from her exertion on the two-mile-or-better walk; she lifted the French plait and fanned her neck. Tendrils of hair were already escaping the braid, framing her lightly freckled face. If she didn't find a ride soon and get out of the sun, there would be a lot more freckles before the day was over.

The sound of an approaching car caused her to turn and look around. She had already let two cars go past without bothering to catch a ride. One had been going too fast; another had been driven by a little old lady who, Tara guessed, was doing good to see the road

much less notice a hitchhiker standing beside it. This
car looked different. It was a station wagon. Even at
this distance Tara could tell that it was occupied by
more than one person. What could be safer than a
family? She decided to defy the fates and test her
whatever-will-be-will-be principle. Hiking her hip toward the highway and sticking out her thumb was too
demeaning, but turning and looking at the car with a
helpless expression wasn't.

The car was moving slowly. Maybe it was slowing.
Maybe . . . It rolled past her, then slowed some more,
pulling onto the shoulder of the road with a crunch of
gravel beneath the tires. Tara limped forward, favor-
ing her blistered foot.

"Having trouble?" the driver asked as he rolled
down the window.

"I'm afraid I am in a bit of a jam," she said, her
voice oozing with charm as she gave the occupants of
the station wagon a dazzling smile. In spite of the three
small faces peering at Tara from the rear seat and the
young woman beside him, the man looked old enough
to be her grandfather. Her heart pounded anxiously as
she advanced toward the car, reminding herself of her
own skirt-chasing grandfather who liked to pinch
women in strategic places.

"I didn't notice a car," the man continued. "Are
you having engine trouble?"

"No, sir," Tara said, stopping beside his door. "I'm
not. My boyfriend and I just had our first argument.
I asked him to let me out of the car." She raised her
hand to the cloud and sighed, asking forgiveness for
stretching the truth. "Honestly, if I have to walk all of
the way to Kathmandu, I will, just to get away from
him."

"Kathmandu," the man said, scratching his head and frowning. "Is that some place in north Mississippi? I haven't heard of it."

Tara smiled. She should have thought to say Jackson or Laurel, something these nicer country folks could identify with instead of a destination halfway around the world. As good as the University of Southern Mississippi was in Hattiesburg, sometimes she forgot that she was no longer in the cosmopolitan center of the universe. "A little past there," she answered.

"Hop in the car, honey," the woman encouraged, and leaned over the backseat to tell her kids, "Unlock the door for the lady. And keep your grubby hands to yourself."

Tara got into the backseat with the three children, who regarded her gravely. Setting her bag at her feet, she slammed the door as the man drove back onto the highway.

"We live in Laurel," the woman explained. "Was that where you were going?"

"Laurel is fine," Tara said. "Would it be too much trouble to take the interstate and drop me before we get into the city?"

"No trouble at all," the man answered. "You just say when."

"Thanks." Tara smiled at the children, who were eyeing her curiously. "Hi," she said, wondering if the little angels ever did anything but stare. "What's your name?" If they were guard dogs, Tara would have worried from the look they gave her. "My name's Tara."

"Tell the lady your name," their mother ordered, and explained for Tara's benefit, "We keep preaching to them not to talk to strangers. Guess that's why they're acting so shy right now. Tell the lady your name," she urged them again. One by one they announced their first names, but the intense stares never lessened.

As they approached Laurel's first exit, Tara peered out the window and looked at the scattered clouds marring the blue sky. "Would you mind dropping me here?" she asked.

"Here?" The man slowed the car and stopped on the shoulder of the highway. There wasn't even a house that he could see nearby, but if the lady wanted out, he would let her be.

"This is perfect," Tara said, climbing out of the car. "You've been wonderful to go out of your way to drop me off." She stood back and waved as the man put the car in gear and headed onto the highway. She took a deep breath before shouldering her lightweight bag. It had only been a short walk from the interstate junction to Laurel's municipal airport, where she sat now anxiously waiting for her next ride.

Tara checked the skies again. Since she'd been sitting there, nothing but a chicken that had escaped from a nearby processing plant had flapped or flown into the little airport. She began to think she should be staking out her next hitchhiking ride in a bigger airport; but she had ruled out Pinebelt Regional because of the commercial air traffic. Just as the hands of the wall clock crossed into another hour, the small airport's radio squawked to life. Tara sat straighter, straining to make some sense of the transmission coming from the adjoining room. Apprehension mingled with excitement. This could be the beginning of step two of her master plan. Applying her psychological training, she assessed the pros and cons of her idea. Would she be safer with a strange pilot than she might be with a strange driver of a car? Planes were more expensive than cars—that alone should indicate a higher class of traveler.

Planes were also used more frequently in illicit operations, she remembered; carrying drugs, for instance. Just last fall she recalled a big news story of a plane loaded with marijuana abandoned at this airport after a forced landing. How was she going to judge if the pilot she chose to fly with wasn't one carrying a high-priced booty of drugs?

The possibilities and the problems made Tara wish she was waiting for a bus instead of an airplane. She should have taken time to think thoroughly through this scheme. But at the time she had envisioned herself cooling her heels in an airplane more easily than she had seen herself swabbing tired feet in a muddy streambed. That was for the birds and Dick Shaw.

Sure, if she could get a ride, she could go a greater distance. But she was taking a bigger risk, and that distance started to worry her. Suppose she was taken somewhere where she couldn't be found? This wasn't like a commercial flight where she would be met at the other end. With a private pilot, there was no telling where she would end up, and no one would be checking if she didn't come home tonight.

That was precisely why she had thought of the airplane for hitchhiking in the first place, she reminded herself. Where was her spirit of adventure and love of challenge? Whatever had happened to her *que será será* attitude?

Even before she had fully worked through her fears over her intended travel plan, Tara overheard the radio operator talking with the pilot. A lot of the jargon didn't make sense, but one thing was clear—the plane seemed to be having some kind of trouble. Tara listened tensely, her eyes scouring the skies for a sign of the aircraft.

It first appeared as a speck above the trees, then grew larger in the sky. The plane approached the runway, positioned itself above the striped markings, and the two main wheels skidded, bumped, touched down again and licked the runway as the nose wheel lowered into place. Tara felt herself breathing again as the plane zipped down the runway. She could tell the pilot had the plane under control; its speed decreased. Then it made a turn off of the runway and taxied toward the airport building.

"What a beauty. That pilot knows his stuff. Looks like he touched down smack dab on the center line and kept her there." Tara noticed a sheen of sweat on the radio operator's forehead. In her concentration on the plane, she hadn't noticed when he had joined her at the doorway.

Tara's lips wavered into a smile. If she was going to beg a ride in that plane, she hoped the pilot was as good at keeping it in the air as he was at maneuvering it on the ground. "What do you think the problem was?" she asked.

"Instrument malfunction or miscalculation," he answered. "He was flying lower than he thought he was." The radio operator stepped outside. Tara followed him to the strip where the corporate jet was parked.

The steps of the aircraft lowered to the ground, but it was several minutes before anyone appeared. The first to emerge was a man, lean and tanned. The way the wind disturbed his hair reminded her of Rick and his shaggy haircut. He might even be classed as handsome, Tara thought, if he didn't look so angry. A classic example of stress, she summed him up, deciding he was probably as good at causing it as having it. As if to confirm her snap evaluation, he demanded, "Where the hell are we?" Sunlight glinting off the frame of his designer sunglasses turned his glare into inquisition.

Hadn't he filed a flight plan, Tara wondered? Shouldn't he know where they were flying, and landing? "Welcome to Laurel, Mississippi," the radio operator greeted. Two men appeared at the head of the steps, but Tara kept her attention riveted on the man at the bottom. Although she hadn't spoken, he continued to level his gaze at Tara as if he expected her to grow into a palm tree if he looked at her long enough. She glanced away and with her practiced eye mentally categorized each man.

A muscle was pulsing in Marcus Landry's temple from the tension of keeping his temper in check. Damn George for getting them off course. Flying at an altitude entirely different from what they believed, they could have crashed head-on into some unsuspecting aircraft. He could still see beads of sweat on George's forehead from the moment he had realized the error and the danger inherent in their position. Damn Paul Redding even more, Marcus thought, projecting his anger now where it rightly belonged, with their employer. If Paul Redding took care of his own responsibilities instead of shoveling them onto someone else, like his cousin, then George could concentrate on the job at hand—flying, in this case.

"What the hell are we doing here?" Paul shouted up the stairway.

George was still too shaken to reply, so Marcus answered, "We got off course."

"Couldn't you have corrected that without landing here in, in—Mississippi, of all places!"

"It's not an easy matter to fix when you don't know where you are," Marcus said calmly. "We had to land to straighten out the flight miscalculations."

"You mean we were lost?" Paul chided. "Is this what I pay you for?" Marcus let the question pass. Paul liked to bait him. Right now Marcus knew how close he was to telling his employer exactly what he thought of him. The muscle pulsed more rapidly at his temple. "Why wasn't I informed?"

"We're informing you now," Marcus returned. "We landed as quickly as we could after discovering the error. We need a few minutes to reset the instruments and we'll be able to take off shortly and get back on course."

"Unless for the last hour we've been flying exactly opposite of where we want to go," Paul griped.

"I checked the flight instruments during the run-up," George spoke up, not wanting Marcus to take the blame when it was his fault they were off course. He didn't add what Marcus already knew, that he had been so preoccupied catering to Paul's last-minute demands he had fed incorrect data into the system.

"How did this happen?" Paul grilled.

"When you're ready for your first flight lesson, I'll be happy to explain it to you in detail," Marcus offered. Experience had taught him that Paul cared nothing for details in his own business much less how they related to someone else's job. Paul liked to command center stage, because it appeared to give him more power; but if that was all Paul had gotten out of a college degree, Marcus didn't think he was missing much. Marcus glanced past Paul's shoulder to the red-haired woman standing in rapture at Paul's feet. It never failed, Marcus thought; wherever Paul went, beautiful women materialized out of nowhere to meet him.

Tara's eyes clashed with the pilot's as he caught her in the act of analyzing him. She felt the intensity of his gaze; it was as if he had reached out and touched her. Wind ruffled his sandy-brown hair, adding to his youthful appearance. His cheeks were lean beneath high cheekbones, giving his face an angularity. Tara admired his effort to control his anger, guessing it was a habit he had perfected. This man might not be the one who was in charge, but he was definitely the one in control. The executive, fuming with impatience, was also aware of the younger man's ability and his own dependence on him, although Tara knew he would never admit it. What a fascinating threesome, she thought, sensing the undercurrents of tension binding them together.

One thing had become clear to her. The airplane's problem appeared to be minor, which fueled her initial intention of asking for a ride. But she wished she could make her request of the pilot instead of going through diplomatic channels with the fuming executive to get results. Ego, she thought, makes for such an interesting study.

"Well, fix it, whatever it takes, so we can get going again," the executive ordered his pilots. "We've lost enough time as it is. I'm going to phone the office and make sure they change our appointments in light of this delay.'' He spun around, speaking in the same arrogant tone, as if the airport radio operator were under his employment. "Where's the phone?"

"This way, sir." The man beside Tara turned to lead the way. After a final glare at the pilots, the executive stalked away from the plane. The escaped chicken that was pecking in the dirt beside the airport building squawked and flapped its wings to get out of the man's way. As Tara looked longingly at the plane, inside which the pilots had already disappeared, she wondered if the turkey buzzard was still eyeing Dick as an entrée beside the road.

All he can do is say, no, she thought, wishing she were asking for her next ride from anyone but a man who reminded her so much of Dick Shaw and her ex-husband.

In the waiting room, even if Tara hadn't wanted to listen in on his conversation, it would have been difficult not to. Apparently his connection was bad. Tara turned her back on him out of respect for his privacy, but her ears perked up immediately. He was changing a whole series of meetings due to the interruption of the flight. And the first destination was somewhere in Virginia.

Virginia would look terrific on a postcard, Tara thought. She would be a heroine in the eyes of the other students if she could wrangle a ride on that airplane. Then she would be an accepted member of the graduate clique, not only to have beaten Dick at his own game but to have done it with her usual flair.

Behind her, the executive hung up the phone. Piecing together his conversation, she determined that he dealt in high finance or had something to do with accounting. His leather soles were mute against the linoleum as he stepped away from the phone. To Tara, it was as if destiny were walking toward her. She turned and smiled. "I couldn't help overhearing—" she began. When he cut those direct light blue eyes at her, she said, "Bad connection?"

His eyes thoroughly devoured her, and Tara let him look. She could tell it was a behavioral method he used in business to get the upper hand, but it wouldn't work with her. She had learned all about body language from her field of study. When he had completed his inspection and realized his search-and-annoy stare was having no noticeable effect on her, he laughed. Tara didn't like the way he delayed his reaction. She had run into men like him before: they laughed at their own jokes, had a standard number of lines they fed every woman they met, and half the time they didn't even listen to what you were saying as they calculated the best method of using you.

"You don't look like you belong here," he said finally. "Do you work here?"

Out of the corner of her eye, Tara noticed the airport's radio operator taking in every word of the exchange. "I'm waiting for a ride," she said nonchalantly, watching the executive with as much scrutiny as he had just given her. "In an airplane," she added, letting that information sink in before she slid in the last detail. "Like yours, for instance." Although he continued to stare at her, she forced herself to stand straight, trying not to back down from the way his eyes bore into hers. With the last of her pent-up breath, she finished, "If it ever flies again."

"It'll fly again," he assured her. "I've paid good money to make certain of that."

Tara smiled then, tired of the game of power cha-rades. "Good," she said, "because I was hoping you might be able to help me."

"Oh?" The frown that had earlier signaled anger now expressed curiosity. "How's that?"

"You're heading in my direction."

"Am I? And where exactly is that?"

"Anywhere," she answered. "I'm not choosy."

The frown deepened; then he laughed as if it were an afterthought. "Did someone put you up to this?"

"Of course not. I make my own decisions. Let me explain."

"By all means," he said, folding his arms across his pin-striped jacket.

"I'm in a contest," she began, "a hitchhiking con-test. It doesn't matter where I go or how I get there. I just have to get farther than my opponent. The only way I figured I could do that was to take a few air-plane rides while my opponent is thinking of a pedes-trian level. Yours is the first plane that's been in here all day. That's why I was hoping you could give me a ride." Knowing that it would annoy him to give the other man more importance but also might just add that edge she needed, she added, "That is, of course, if your pilot wouldn't think an extra passenger would create a problem."

The stranger with the airplane laughed, this time more spontaneously, something Tara didn't think happened often. The sound didn't make her feel any more relaxed. "I don't pay my pilot to think," he re-sponded. "Marcus Landry does what I tell him to do if he wants to keep his job."

"Then you wouldn't mind if I came along, just for the ride, Mr.—?" She pressed her advantage, pleased that he had played right into her hands. If anyone had his head in the clouds, she thought, it was this man, not the pilot.

"Paul Redding," he introduced himself. "And I'd be delighted," he said, turning on the charm, "especially if we get lost again."

But Tara thought of the pilot's piercing blue eyes and didn't think he was the type of man who would make the same mistake twice.

Chapter Two

Dear Julie:

Only got as far as Norfolk, Virginia, on the first day. But I won't complain, since I arrived early enough to attend a party on a yacht. The Chesapeake Bay at dusk is highly romantic. Do you think Dick would mind if I add nautical miles into the day's hitchhiking total?

Smooth sailing,

Tara

This is a dream, Tara thought, standing on the deck of an eighty-foot yacht and watching the sunset. Concentrating on the champagne glass in her hand, she wondered if she were imagining the setting. She had been drinking champagne the night of the end-of-semester party, too. Perhaps she was still at *that* party and had had too much to drink. She might wake up in the morning with a hangover and find she was still in Hattiesburg, Mississippi, still facing stacks of psychology books that appeared to grow taller with every one she read.

A glass shattered behind her. Tara turned as a deck steward appeared out of nowhere to clear away the debris. The woman who had dropped the glass stepped over the shards and reached for a fresh drink from a passing waiter. The woman's gold-strap high heels reminded Tara of her own limited wardrobe, although some guests were barefoot and wearing barely more than a bikini.

Tara shook her head. The beautiful people, Paul Redding's clients, people so rich their accountant, Paul, flew to their yachts, homes and islands to take care of their minor business and tax details. Paul had taken great pains to impress her during the flight to Norfolk. He had played up his importance in the CPA firm he headed in Texas, had dropped names like Hunt and Libby, which meant little more than canned-goods labels to Tara, and she had told him that, piquing him more because she had been less impressed. She turned her back on the laughter and took courage from the setting sun, watching it turn the waters of Chesapeake Bay golden. How far had Dick gotten in fourteen hours? Smiling to herself, she spread her arms along the rails as if she owned the yacht and thought of all that had happened in such a short time.

After Paul had agreed to let her hitch a flight, George Redding, the copilot, had entered the airport waiting room to tell Paul they were ready to leave. George was slightly pudgy, with a face still red from the circumstances behind the airplane's unscheduled landing. He didn't appear surprised to learn that Paul had picked up an extra passenger. Tara couldn't help wondering if the pilot would feel the same way.

George's reaction alerted Tara to expect Paul to turn amorous once they were airborne. True to form, it was only moments after the pilot announced seat belts could be unbuckled that Paul went into action. Tara spent the remainder of the flight keeping her host in his place, thankful for all of the practice she had had with Dick Shaw.

When they landed in Norfolk, Tara booked a room in the same hotel where the Redding cousins and Marcus Landry were spending the night. On the taxi ride, Paul, who went ahead of the pilot and copilot, had invited Tara to join them for dinner on the yacht. "My clients always invite so many people; one more person won't sink the ship," he had said. At first Tara had refused, anxious only for relief from his arrogance, but when she thought of Dick and how good a yachting cruise would look on her first postcard, she let Paul think he had charmed her into accepting the invitation.

The party certainly gave her material for one line of a postcard, she thought now, but very little else. Observing George Redding had amused Tara for a while. He had stalked the waiters with the hors d'oeuvre trays, choosing nibbles from each so that no one waiter would realize how much he consumed. But Paul Redding's friends were empty, concerned only with their narrow world of existence and how it related to the almighty dollar. Tara sighed, wishing she could swim ashore and get a good night's sleep before beginning the airport hitchhiking sequence all over again in the morning. Turning, she spied Marcus Landry, the pilot, leaning negligently against the rail of the yacht, looking out to sea.

She hadn't seen him again until they shared a taxi to the harbor that evening, and even then he hadn't spoken a word on the drive. Since their arrival on the yacht, he had kept to himself at the stern of the boat while Paul had made the rounds, introducing Tara to his friends. When Paul began entertaining his clients with his version of Tara's hitchhiking story, she had slipped unnoticed from his side. Marcus had made no effort to join the others. Now Tara realized he probably felt he didn't belong here any more than she did. On impulse, she joined him at the rail.

Sensing someone standing nearby, Marcus turned. Her again, he thought. She kept turning up underfoot just when he managed to get her out of his thoughts—although that wasn't perfectly accurate this evening, since he had managed to keep her in his line of sight from the moment they had come aboard. He didn't usually take such interest in Paul's arm decorations, but something about this woman was different. From the moment he had set eyes on her at the airport that afternoon, he had been struck by the openness of her gaze. She was like a sponge, absorbing everything around her, even when it was none of her business. Her eyes had told him she had seen right through his mask that afternoon, sensing with some uncanny intuition how close to boiling his anger had been. If she hadn't been standing at the foot of the airplane's steps, a witness to his actions, there was no telling where he'd be right now or whom Paul would have found to replace him. Marcus couldn't decide if he was grateful that she had unwittingly acted as a check on his temper or not. Like it or not, he needed this job until he could qualify for another one. Without a high-flying degree behind his name, as Paul and George had, he couldn't be choosy in the job market. "Paul just went below," Marcus told her.

"I noticed," Tara answered, and smiled as she added, "Thank goodness."

Marcus's eyebrows perked up. What was her game, he wondered? Was she planning to use Marcus for some sort of jealousy display? That afternoon, just as Marcus had gotten his mind back on the flight plan, she had turned up again, as an extra passenger. It still amazed Marcus how Paul had managed to talk such an intelligent-looking woman into joining his mile-high club on the spur of the moment, especially after such an unlikely landing in Laurel, Mississippi. *It's such a waste,* he thought softening momentarily. *Like throwing her to the lions.* He regained control over his emotions, telling himself it was no less than she deserved if she could be attracted to Paul's superficiality.

Her eyes snared him. Up close now, he could see they were deep green with gold flecks, but there was more, something almost indefinable, like a glow emanating from her through those all-seeing, yet sensitive eyes. He felt his pulse quicken and almost looked away, but mesmerized, he continued to stare at her. There was a softness about her, too, the way her hair framed her lightly freckled face, making him think of a woman-child, utterly feminine, even when she had worn her hair pulled back in that twist earlier today. Tonight her hair was free and loose, and he had to fight an urge to weave his fingers into the burnished strands.

Marcus could tell she was aware of his questions— who she was and where she fit into this crowd. Her eyes remained linked with his as she smiled and asked, "Are you having a good time?"

"Paul doesn't pay me to have a good time," he answered in clipped tones. *Remember your place,* he reminded himself. *She's out of your league.*

"Paul is a bore," she stated, and looked away from him. They had barely spoken ten words to each other since their meeting; it made no sense that she felt nervous in his presence. But she hadn't been able to forget the look he had given her the first time he had set eyes on her. Seeing him standing alone just now had given her heart another minor tremor. Marcus's glances were more potent than Paul's knee nonchalantly brushing hers in the cabin of the airplane. "In other words, you wouldn't be here if it weren't part of your job."

She was much more intelligent than Paul realized, Marcus decided. He wondered what she was after, since she had obviously already grown tired of Paul's brand of fun and games. "I wouldn't be here tonight," he clarified, "if it were not for you. Paul seemed to think we had to make this a command performance."

"Sorry," she said, and shivered slightly in the gusty breeze. For all of his tight-lipped silence, he was a difficult man to ignore. Something about him made her very much aware of his masculinity, especially when they were standing so close. It was as if they communicated with each other without words. The message, however, was one Tara didn't completely understand, and that unnerved her, because she was usually so good at assessing character. But Marcus Landry defied all of her known categories of men.

This one is different, he told himself again, and wished he had the opportunity and time to figure out why. Something about her reeked of class. It was in the way she carried herself, what she wore, the inflection in her voice. Yet there was also something entirely earthy about her, exotic but at the same time innocent. "You don't look like a small-town girl." He wanted to keep his distance, but he kept feeling drawn to her warmth. She was like a beautiful but deadly cobra, mesmerizing him with her sensuality, waiting for the moment to strike. The funny thing was, she didn't seem aware of her potency—or else she was all too aware, and that was how she caught men in her spell.

She looked down at the dress of Indian cotton that she had brought along because it rolled up and packed well in a suitcase. "My dress doesn't give me away?" She smiled. The way he was looking at her made her feel as if she were wearing a gown of spun gold.

The fairness of her skin made her look as if she were blushing. It made her even more engaging. "You could be wearing an outfit straight out of Dogpatch," he lazily drawled, liking her in spite of warnings to himself not to, "and you'd still have that stamp of society intelligence about you."

Tara didn't know whether to feel offended or flattered. "Do only people from big cities look that way?"

He shrugged. He had come from the city himself, but he hadn't been recognized by "society." "You just don't look like somebody from Mississippi."

"Hey," she said, smiling as she thought that he might lighten up if she did, "don't knock the place unless you've lived there. It happens to be home for me right now, and I like it."

"But you haven't always lived there," he guessed. His eyes met hers. He felt a sudden urge to know everything about her, from her earliest childhood memories to the moment they had met. And he didn't want the knowledge to end there. *What a romantic,* he thought, clamping down on his emotions. He turned away from her, leaning on the rail of the yacht, watching the moon rise. *It's the full moon making you act so crazy.*

Words caught in Tara's throat as his eyes held hers for one intense moment before he looked away. Suddenly she realized *he* was the reason she had come tonight. It had nothing to do with Paul Redding's invitation to join a party on a yacht or how good the news of that would look on a postcard. Marcus Landry, with his probing blue eyes, had been the draw.

"No," she admitted, leaning on the rail and sharing the sight of the moon with him. "You're right." The sky was still flaming orange in afterglow from the sunset. A breeze lifted her hair. A gull cried nearby. Tara inhaled the sea air and thought how much it made her miss her condo on the Cape. She looked at him, wondering how much else he had guessed about her. "Boston was my home until recently."

"Boston?" A glimmer of a smile turned up one corner of his mouth. "From Boston to Mississippi?" It reminded him of his own beginnings, from a small city in Pennsylvania to the money mecca of Texas. Somehow he didn't think that money had led her to Mississippi.

Tara turned, resting her back against the ship's railing. She slanted her eyes in his direction. "I suppose it does sound odd. The first night I flew in, I didn't even know where Mississippi was on the map, much less Hattiesburg." She took a deep breath of the tangy sea air. "I've lived there almost a year now, and

I like the place. It's small enough to drive just about anywhere in ten or fifteen minutes. I've almost forgotten how long it takes to go from the shore into Boston. Hattiesburg is close to New Orleans, the Gulf Coast, Jackson and Mobile—if I feel the need for nightlife.''

Marcus could imagine her feeling that need often. She was the kind of woman who fit in with Paul's crowd, partying on yachts, skinny-dipping until dawn, flying off to nowhere at the drop of a suggestion. And what they did in-flight—He censored his thoughts before his anger mushroomed again. Whatever her motives for accepting Paul's offer of a ride, Marcus found himself enjoying talking to her. "Is Hattiesburg famous for anything?" he asked, to avoid imagining her falling into Paul's arms the way the others did.

"Not that I'm aware of," she answered, sipping her champagne, considering his question. She smiled at him. "Except for the fact that it's where I live."

"That's a noteworthy point." Something about her didn't connect with Paul. It was as if she saw through Paul's shenanigans and was using *him* instead of the other way around. Marcus's eyes softened as he returned Tara's glance. He watched the breeze ruffling her hair and resisted the urge to reach out and tuck a stray lock in place. "Something important must have led you to Mississippi."

Tara nodded and looked away from him. He stirred something within her that made her unable to sustain his gaze for any length of time. And yet he kept drawing her back for look after look. "I've gone back to school."

"Really?" he said, revealing a smile that made her catch her breath. "No kidding." Excitement rippled through his voice. "In Mississippi?" He was tempted to tell her how he'd toyed with the idea of completing his education. It wouldn't take that long. He'd already checked into the requirements. But with his erratic schedule flying Paul around the world at the drop of a hat, he didn't have the time to settle into a consistent routine. But to meet this sophisticated woman who was actually following through with his dream made Marcus feel a kinship with her. If she could do it, maybe it wasn't so ridiculous for a man of his age to complete high school. "Why Mississippi? Why not Boston?"

"The University of Southern Mississippi happens to have one of the best clinical psychology departments in the nation. I'm working on my doctoral degree."

His smile vanished. "A doctor's degree." Thank God he hadn't told her how few classes he lacked to finish high school. Dreams of a correspondence course just wouldn't stack up to a doctor's degree. She probably would have doubled over laughing and then run straight to Paul with the information. Marcus cut short a laugh. *She's not for you,* he told himself, turning away. *That education is what makes her different.* He turned away.

"Ph.D.," she corrected with a laugh, realizing for the first time that day how nice it was to be free of study for a few weeks. She wondered if he had overheard Paul's explanation of her hitchhiking story; he had certainly told the tale often enough. Tara wanted to set the record straight with Marcus, and she was about to explain why she had talked Paul into giving her a ride in the airplane when she realized that instead of talking about herself, she wanted to know more about Marcus. "Where are you from, Marcus?"

"Allentown."

"Pennsylvania?"

"Yes."

"Big family or little?" It was a question she liked to ask in counseling sessions. She learned a lot about a person from his background.

"Average."

Tara stared at Marcus. Even in profile his face had a modeled look, like a work of art. His cheeks looked so smooth she wondered if he ever had problems shaving. Something had changed between them. Just when she had felt he was opening up to her, he had suddenly retreated into his shell, like a hermit crab threatened by a predator. She wondered if he felt she was probing by asking about his family, so she tried a different tactic. "Have you always been a pilot?"

"No, I was a baby before that." Where were all of these questions leading? Was she searching for something to laugh about with Paul later? Why tell her all of the odd jobs he had held trying to support first his family, then a teenage wife, while he spent every free hour learning to fly with barnstorming pilots? Flying was the only way he had seen to better himself when he couldn't find the time to finish his education, and his ex-wife had taken every opportunity to remind him he would never be a success because of it.

She stared at him for a moment longer, wondering what she had said that had caused his change in attitude. It annoyed her to think she had somehow been insensitive when she prided herself on her professional nurturing skills. "I'm sorry if my questions offended you," she said, stiffening her shoulders. "I didn't mean to pry." She finished the last of her champagne and looked around for the waiter with the tray of drinks.

Damn, he thought, *now I've made her mad.* He wondered whether he should apologize but wasn't quite sure how to go about it without embarrassing himself. A gong sounded, announcing dinner. *Saved by the bell,* he thought, but couldn't decide if he was happy to have an excuse to avoid her questions or sad to end the opportunity to talk to her.

Tara turned to Marcus, wanting to say more, wishing they weren't parting on such a strained note, but his look was hooded against her.

"We'd better go in," he said. "We wouldn't want to commit a social sin and be late. Are you ready?"

"No," she answered. She wouldn't mind missing the meal if she thought she could learn more about Marcus Landry. She had just begun to scratch the surface of his personality and hadn't made much of a mark. He was too hard, like a diamond in the rough. "But I suppose it's expected."

Marcus finished his glass of Perrier and dumped the ice and slice of lime over the rail. "Unless someone needs a glass of wine refilled or your pretty face to look at, I don't think either of us would be greatly missed. But the empty place setting in the formal seatings wouldn't be overlooked." He had learned something about protocol during his work for Paul; some things didn't have to be learned from a book.

His compliment warmed her even as the sea breeze chilled her. It was the way he had said she was pretty, as if he resented it but accepted it as fact. She knew that it would be useless to try to get him to open up to

her when she could tell he had set his mind against exchanging further intimacies with her. What nerve had
she touched?

Tara couldn't remember ever having sat through a
more boring meal. She found herself eating everything on her plate—even eyeing the parsley out of
monotony. She tried to strike up a conversation with
the people seated on either side of her, but all of her
overtures didn't elicit further responses. It was as if
talking was more effort than they cared to expend.

Dessert arrived; then cordials were taken out onto
the deck and into other rooms of the luxury ship as
everyone moved away from the formal banquet table.
Tara was grateful that she wasn't wearing a watch. The
evening would have passed more slowly if she had
been aware of how much time dragged.

Eventually, she noticed her host asking Paul when
he was leaving. It surprised her to hear Paul ask Marcus for the answer. "Six in the morning," Marcus said
with his succinct style.

Tara suppressed a smile. She couldn't imagine Paul
getting up for anything before noon, especially after
all of the liquor he had consumed. Marcus had kept to
his Perrier all evening. She had thought it must be
torture to be so sober in this tiresome crowd.

Tara found it difficult staying awake on the ride
back to the hotel. George, having eaten well, looked
drowsy, too. She wanted to talk to Marcus, but not
with Paul breathing down her shoulder. Besides, once
they were settled in the taxi, Marcus leaned his head
against the back of the seat and closed his eyes. It was
as effective as hanging out a Do Not Disturb sign.
Paul was the only one who acted as if he had been
drinking nothing but black coffee all evening, and he

kept eyeing her all the way back to the Hilton. Tara didn't mind sharing a ride, but she had no intentions of sharing anything else with Paul Redding. The way he was looking at her made her glad they would be parting company when the taxi ride ended.

When they arrived at the hotel, Marcus dealt with the driver and the tip. Yawning, George told everyone good-night and toddled off to his room. Tara walked through the lobby doors, lingering casually as she waited for Marcus to catch up with her so that she could tell him goodbye. She looked through the glass doorways at him, thinking how handsome he was.

Not wanting to be obvious, she walked over to the reception desk and picked up a postcard depicting the Hilton. She still had to send something to Julie to prove she had gotten this far the first day. Otherwise, who would believe her? She smiled as she gave half a thought to Dick and pictured him curled up next to his backpack trying to get comfortable for the night in a ditch beside the road. She wouldn't be at all surprised if the turkey vulture from that morning was still keeping him company.

Paul joined her at the desk. "It was a lovely evening, Paul." Tara mouthed the words she knew he expected to hear, and she tried to sound gracious. "I can't thank you enough for giving me a lift out of Mississippi this morning. It's given me a head start on my game plan."

"It was entirely my pleasure," he replied, giving her his charming-host smile. "But it doesn't have to end there. Why don't you come with us tomorrow?"

Glancing at the night clerk, Tara moved away so that they wouldn't be overheard. She had had half a mind to ask Paul if she could continue on the flight with them. But she didn't want to feel too indebted to anyone, particularly a man like Paul Redding. He might easily get the idea she owed him much more than plane fare in exchange for a free ride. "You've done enough already. I'm truly grateful." On the other hand, it would simplify her strategy if she didn't have to waste time day after day looking for new rides in each place she landed. That would give her more time to search for exotic picture postcards to mail home.

"You made the trip less monotonous. There's room on the airplane, so why not continue on with us?"

"I wouldn't want you to go to any trouble on my account," she said. Out of the corner of her eye she noticed Marcus enter the hotel. He glanced briefly at both of them and headed for the elevators. Tara wanted to call out to him, but she didn't want to be rude to Paul. Why bother, she asked herself. They would never see each other again.

"You haven't been a bit of trouble," Paul said. "In fact, you were the only bright spot that came out of that unscheduled landing."

"It was my good fortune that you came along when you did." By now, Dick probably wished he hadn't brought so many things in his backpack. Tara was wishing she had packed more, like high heels and a formal dress or a swimsuit. While she was sunning and building up a tan, drinking champagne and mingling with high society at yacht parties, Dick would be choking on exhaust fumes and scratching from chigger bites. She could already picture the banners her classmates would prepare for her triumphant return. Accepting another ride with Paul was tempting, because it made things so easy.

"Come with us tomorrow," he urged. "We're going to Bermuda. That would look pretty impressive for this contest of yours, wouldn't it?"

"It might," she agreed, acting as if the thought didn't really interest her. What if she got stuck in Bermuda and Paul left her behind? An island wouldn't be as easy to get off of as a city on mainland America. The longer they drew out their association, the less guarantees she had that she could keep Paul Redding in line. His knee rubbing from the flight that afternoon had made it obvious where his intentions lay. "Where are you going after that?"

"How does Europe sound?"

"Expensive," she said, all of her defenses firmly in place. She wanted to be certain he knew that she wasn't agreeing to anything but occupancy of one of his airplane's seats. *If* she agreed. And if she accepted, she wanted to feel as if she were in control, not under Paul's power. She looked toward the elevator that Marcus had taken and watched the lights stop on the fourth floor.

"It needn't be," he said. "I can easily write you off on my expense account. It's a simple matter of giving you the proper label."

"That label wouldn't happen to be 'mistress,' would it?" she asked, wondering if anyone in the lobby could overhear them. She lowered her chin like a bull ready to charge and leveled her eyes at him.

"Not at all," he said. "I'm simply inviting you to be my companion as long as the destinations interest you. No strings, if you don't want them," he added.

Tara was thinking of the miles. Bermuda, while it was in the Atlantic Ocean, wasn't too great a distance from Mississippi. Dick Shaw could easily equal the same amount of land miles heading west by taking highways. But she didn't know Paul Redding well enough to trust in what he was offering her, strings or no strings.

"After Bermuda, we're flying to London," he said to influence her decision.

Mentally, Tara pictured that on the map. It would add more miles, a *lot* more miles, if she had better than Bermuda Triangle luck with Paul, but that was part of the risk she had taken in agreeing to this contest. She kept thinking of all of the kids who had bet their hard-earned money on her winning this contest. And what if Dick had guessed her strategy?

"I have to see a client who's vacationing in Kent," he continued. "There's an English garden party we'll be attending. English gardens are lovely this time of the year. You'll fit right in with all of the other flowers."

Tara tried to keep a smile on her face. His flattery bothered her; it was too pat. "English gardens are lovely any time of the year," she commented. "It's the Gulf Stream that keeps the country relatively warm most of the year. And the English, like most of the Europeans I've known, love their gardens."

"You've been to England?"

"Yes." She folded her arms across her chest and tapped her toe against the floor, hoping her attitude of disinterest would make him more eager to take her with him on *her* terms. "Tell me more." She wanted to be talked into staying with him for the duration of the plane ride. She had an overwhelming desire to beat Dick Shaw soundly, and it would be a piece of tea cake and English scones with the aid of an airplane. But she still wasn't convinced she wanted to be under that much of an obligation to one person, especially when that person was Paul Redding.

"From there we'll be flying to Norway, into Bergen."

"That's a pretty good hop," Tara said. She wished she had a map to calculate the miles. Surely Dick wouldn't be able to come anywhere near that kind of track record.

"I have a client who owns a small lodge on a fjord at Flåm. He spends his summers there and his winters in Texas."

Tara didn't wait for Paul to give her the selling point that most appealed to her. "This is the time for the midnight sun. I've always wanted to visit them."

"I wouldn't want to tour Norway in the dead of winter," he said. "All of that darkness could get very depressing, not to mention the cold. As it is, it could get pretty cold this time of the year, especially at night. We might have to buy a warm sweater for you."

"I can buy my own clothes, thank you," she said. "Do you make these grand tours of Europe often?"

He straightened his tie, obviously proud of what he did for a living. "Once or twice a year, perhaps. It depends on the needs of our clients and how their business concerns change throughout the year. What we try to do is group several together for one big sweep, as we did this time. I'm only sorry I can't offer you a free hotel room, as well—at least not until Norway, when we'll be guests of my client."

She *bet* he was sorry about that. "What about the return flight?" she asked without a frown. "Suppose I did agree to accept your generous offer—how close to Mississippi could you take me to drop me off on the return?"

"We could fly you back to Laurel as easily as any other place," he said. "It's on the way to Houston."

Tara considered that a moment, then asked, "Are you going anywhere after Norway?"

"We'll be flying into Luxembourg," he said. "I have a client who is staying in the northern part of the country, in the Ardennes. It's a little town called Vianden. Victor Hugo was in exile there."

Tara smiled. It sounded as if that was something he had thrown in to impress her. He probably didn't know who Victor Hugo was. Why not, she thought, at least for one more day. She could always bail out if Paul's advances got too hot to handle. "As long as you understand I'm just accepting the ride—"

"No strings," he said, holding up his hands and smiling. With his hands in the air, Tara thought he looked like a puppet. In comparison, it made her aware of Marcus's strength and the sense of control she had felt about him. If Paul got out of hand with her, she'd just use Marcus for a chaperone. But remembering his brooding eyes, she wondered who was going to protect her from Marcus.

"In that case," Tara said, "I guess I'll see you here in the lobby at six tomorrow morning."

Chapter Three

Dear Julie:

I'm going to run out of suntan lotion. The water here in Bermuda looks irresistible. I'll have to buy a new straw hat and bathing suit due to this unexpected detour. But Dick would understand. Those are the breaks with hitchhiking—you have to go where your ride takes you.

Sunnily yours,
Tara

As the plane touched down in the shimmering heat of the airport's runway in Bermuda, Tara could barely conceal her grin. She tried to imagine where Dick might be at that same moment. It was possible he could have gotten as far as the West Coast, if he was lucky or had used his wits, as Tara had. She hoped he hadn't had that foresight. It would be degrading to return home and find that she had endured Paul's less than subtle game of footsie for nothing.

Giving Dick the benefit of the doubt, she mentally placed him in Arizona—hot, dry Arizona—in the middle of the desert, with no sunscreen and no oasis in sight. He'd be baking. Deciding that was a cruel fate for anyone, even Dick Shaw, she instead allowed him a hat and hot, sticky clothes to wear for protection against the sun. She could picture the kind of message he would send today on one of those Last Chance postcards. In a British colony like Bermuda, for instance, one might see signs for the Last Chance Pub or Last Chance Public Beach. In the desert, Dick would only find signs for the Last Chance Gas Station or the Last Chance to See Anything but Cactus.

The plane landed with a light skip of the tires against the runway, increasing Tara's respect for Marcus's ability as a pilot. The sight of palm trees and beaches completely restored her faith in the navigational corrections of the plane. Once the engines were cut and the plane was safely parked with other corporate jets and light aircraft, Marcus and George emerged from the cockpit. "Everything and everyone seems to be functioning properly again," Marcus announced. He glared at Tara as if he would like to find an excuse for her extra weight throwing the plane off balance so that he could eliminate her as a passenger. Tara smiled, determined to make him like her. It wasn't going to be easy after the astonishment he had shown that morning when she had turned up for the next leg of the flight.

"We're going ahead into town," Paul announced to Marcus. "You can follow once you take care of all of the parking fees and tie down the plane." He unbuckled his seat belt and stretched. "We could use a good hot shower right about now."

Marcus caught the sultry inflection in Paul's voice. It was bad enough to spend the entire flight imagining what was happening in the cabin without having

Paul rub it in. His eyes silently questioned Tara, who quickly responded, ''A *cold* shower would be more advisable.'' She smiled sweetly in Paul's direction and was rewarded with the hint of a grin from Marcus. Maybe she was giving Paul much more than he bargained for, Marcus thought.

Tara didn't want *anyone* to get the improper idea about her and had declined Paul's offer to stay in the bungalow provided by his Bermudan client. She wanted to keep their sleeping arrangements clearly separate. Besides, Marcus hadn't been included in the invitation. To make her position—or lack of one— with Paul clearer to everyone, she added, ''It's no inconvenience for me to wait until everything's in order here. I'll ride into town with Marcus.''

He was glad that she wasn't acting on cue like one of Paul's trained pets, but Marcus still couldn't figure out what her motives were where he was concerned. ''It could take awhile,'' Marcus predicted with a look that said it would take a lot longer if she stayed behind and got in his way.

She couldn't understand why he disliked her. ''Suit yourself,'' she said with an attempt at lightheartedness. ''But I'll still wait with you.'' Again she had the impression that of the three of them, Marcus Landry was the man in control. Paul's blustery businesslike attitude was more an attempt to show his authority than a sign of his leverage. George was little more than a puppy dog responding to his employer's whims.

The clients met Paul and George at the airport and took them to the bungalow, and Tara just waited silently while Marcus finished his chores. She was sure he was taking longer than necessary just because he knew she was waiting, but she kept a smile on her face to spite him and congratulated herself about outfoxing Dick. Who would have guessed that she could get to Bermuda by hitchhiking? Once they were in the taxi, she kept looking for a way to start a conversation with Marcus. Marcus just huddled in his corner, acting as if she would go away if he pretended she didn't exist.

Marcus didn't know how much more he could stand. She was like a chameleon, acting so sweet and innocent when she was near him. But he could lay bets that the naïveté disappeared when she was alone with Paul, who liked the bold and brassy type. Marcus opened his eyes just enough to look at her through half-opened lids. She had to be just like all of Paul's other women. Why else would he keep her around?

Tara glanced at Marcus and realized he had been watching her while pretending to snooze. She gave up trying to be conversational. "Would you mind," she asked in formal tones to let him know she knew he wasn't sleeping, "if we take time to mail a postcard before going to the hotel? I have to prove that I'm here."

"Who needs to know?"

Tara peered at him and thought the question seemed a little more than idly curious. It was the first response she had gotten from him all day. "It's for my roommate, Julie."

"Julie?" he said, his voice full of incredulity.

"Yes, Julie. Why?"

"Somehow I don't picture you with a roommate. Not a female one, anyway."

"I'm sharing a house with her to cut costs while we're both in graduate school. So if you don't mind, could we go to a post office so that I can buy some stamps?''

"I don't mind at all," he said, sliding back against the seat to rest his head against the cushions. "Nothing's too far out of the way from anything in Hamilton. I'll have the driver drop us on Front Street. It'll just be a short walk from there. You don't mind walking, do you?"

"No, not at all," she answered, "as long as it's not halfway across the country." She thought of Dick.

A moped whipped around the taxi, disturbing the icy silence that had built up between them. "Why do you bother to send postcards?" he asked. "You're bound to get home before the cards do."

"Julie's expecting it."

"Oh, I get it. One of those wish-you-were-here cards to let everyone know how the great Paul Redding charmed you into accompanying him on this trip. How he managed it in such a short time is beyond me. But then, he's run into eager, aggressive types like you before who do anything at the wave of a hundred-dollar bill."

Tara faced him. "You have that wrong, Mr. Landry. In the first place, if there was any charm involved—which I assure you there wasn't—I was the charming one."

He grinned. She was even more beautiful when her emotions were aroused. The gold flecks in her green eyes looked like sparks. "I can believe that, almost."

"And," she huffed, "the only thing that appealed to me about Paul Redding was the fact that he had an airplane. It could have belonged to a little old lady from Pascagoula for all I cared."

"A rich little old lady."

"Granted, but I assure you, the airplane is all I care about. My traveling has a purpose to it, and that purpose has nothing to do with charming Mr. Redding, or you, for that matter." She added the last as a statement to herself. What did it matter what this man thought of her? *Don't go losing your professional cool over nothing,* she warned herself.

"Next you'll be telling me you're just along for the ride so that you can see the Redding firm in action before you hand over all of your accounting to the boy wonder himself."

"If there's any wonder in it, I wonder what most people see in the man," she said testily. "He's not my type."

"I find that hard to believe."

"I don't know why. You don't like Paul Redding very much, either, do you?" she asked.

"No."

"Then why work for him?"

He was silent a few moments. Maybe he had gotten the wrong idea about her and Paul. But what other explanation was there? He looked at her hair blowing softly in the breeze from the open window and wanted to reach out and touch it, to caress her hair in his palm and feel its silky softness. He hadn't ever paid so much attention to any of Paul's ladies, nor could he remember ever feeling so tenderly toward his wife. What was it about this woman that tugged at his feelings so? "It was for the money, to begin with," he answered, softening toward her, "and a chance to prove that I could make something of myself."

Tara waited for him to continue. When he didn't, she gently searched for more. "And now?"

"I tell myself I'm going to quit every other day. Once or twice lately, I've come close to telling Paul the same thing. Landing in Mississippi was one of those times."

"You could have fooled me," Tara said. "I knew you were upset, but you were also in control. I would never have guessed you were that close to your limit."

"I don't respect the way the man operates," he said. His eyes pierced hers. "You're a perfect example."

She stiffened as her anger simmered again. "What do you mean by that?"

"It's not unusual for him to charter a plane for, quote, business purposes, unquote, to impress some woman with an overnight trip to Tahoe or Las Vegas or—"

"Bermuda and Europe, right?" she finished for him.

Another penetrating glance was his answer.

"Let me reemphasize that *I* was the one who asked to come along."

"That's what they all say."

She rolled her eyes. "Well, it's not what you're thinking."

"You don't have to try to explain. I can understand how it is. What woman wouldn't ask to be jetted off to some glamorous island and mingle with the very rich like those at last night's yacht party?"

"This woman wouldn't."

"No, of course you wouldn't," he answered sarcastically. "That's why you kicked and screamed and begged to be left behind when you received last night's invitation. Or were you the one to ask Paul to continue the ride?"

Tara fumed. "All right. The party was a bad example." She couldn't tell him that he was the only reason she had wanted to go to the party. Where was the psychologist's rapier wit when it was needed? Why did her mind turn to mush around Marcus when she usually thought like a calculator? She said the first thing that came to mind. "The last few weeks have been intense with my schoolwork. Yesterday had its own tense moments, and by the time the invitation for the party arrived, I was ready for a mindless break. But it's not my normal scene. I don't think it's yours, either, yet you were there." She smiled to herself, pleased that she had ended up turning the question on the questioner. *You might make a good psychologist yet,* she told herself.

"Because of you. I explained that last night."

"Sort of. But—oh, damn," she said, expelling her breath in exasperation. "How can I make you understand that Paul Redding is the antithesis of everything I look for in a man? He has an airplane. It happened to be the only one that had come anywhere near Laurel's airport that day. I needed the plane more than I did him."

Marcus's brows rose jauntily. "As I said before," he continued, "most women are impressed by the plane and all of the trappings that go with Redding." He picked up her hand. "I see he hasn't gone so far as to buy you any trinkets yet."

She snatched her hand back. "And he won't if I have my say in the matter. How can I make you understand?" She glared at him, wondering how she had imagined sensitivity in his blue eyes. Just when she had talked herself into enduring Paul's superficial embraces a little longer in exchange for the convenience

of using his plane to win the hitchhiking contest—
there was no way Dick could possibly make it to England, she hoped—Marcus made the prospect even
more annoying. "I'm just along for the ride. Nothing
else."

"They all say that, too."

"I'm not all."

He frowned, wanting to believe it; but as long as she
was remotely associated with Paul, the evidence was
stacked against her. "If you had some purpose in
going where we're going, I might believe you. But how
could you even have known where we're headed?"

"I didn't need to know where you were going," she
said. "All I had to do was hitch a ride with you. And
I do have a purpose," she said, and sighed. "Maybe I
should start at the beginning. Didn't Paul tell you
about my hitchhiking contest?"

"Paul Redding tells me very little unless it's pre-
ceded by 'Marcus do this,' or, 'Marcus do that.'"

"Well, I'm in a hitchhiking contest," she began.

"Hitchhiking," he said with a skeptical smile.
"And you expect me to believe that? What are you, a
writer who makes up stories out of thin air?"

"No, I'm a psychologist, or will be," she amended,
"once I finish my doctorate."

"That's out of my class, too, and worse," he said.
"I'll have to put a latch on my mind so that you won't
analyze me at random."

"I don't do that," she huffed, "unless there's a fee
for my analysis."

"I can certainly picture you on a couch," he said,
his eyes roaming over her face. "But it wouldn't be for
psychological purposes."

She smiled at him with gritted teeth and turned his previous phrase back on himself. "That's what they all say in my business."

Marcus gracefully acknowledged the put-down and said more quietly, "I still can't picture you as a hitchhiker." Sitting here with her, acting so fresh and alive, it was hard enough for Marcus to imagine her with Paul. There was so much that was contradictory about her.

"Why not?" she demanded. Any other time she would have agreed with him, but she was angry enough now to argue any point with him.

"You hardly look as if you're all thumbs."

She wanted to laugh, but it would destroy all of the worked-up anger. "Hitchhiking isn't easy," she defended. Silently, she wished Dick Shaw would find a hole in the sole of his shoe for getting her into this situation. A week ago she would never have pictured herself defining the merits or pitfalls of hitchhiking to anyone, yet in two days she felt like an expert. "You never know who's going to pick you up—you and Paul Redding are prime examples. You never know how long it's going to take between rides—which was why I was so eager to go with anyone, even Paul, when your plane landed. And you never know where you'll end up being stranded."

"You're right," he said, nodding sadly. "It must be awful to find yourself in Bermuda."

She glared at him, clamped her mouth shut and turned to give the seat upholstery more consideration than Marcus Landry deserved.

Silence drew out between them. The driver slowed the taxi as the traffic thickened, and they entered bustling Front Street, where shops carrying English goods, antiques, crystal and woolens attracted her attention. On the opposite side of the street, monstrous cruise ships were docked on the quay. Tara wanted to crane her neck out the window for a better view, anxious to see all of Bermuda at once, but she didn't want to act like a typical tourist in front of Marcus.

"You can let us off here," Marcus said, leaning forward to speak to the driver as a bottleneck of traffic kept them stationary for several minutes. He paid the driver in Bermudan currency, then leaned across Tara to open the door on her side, away from the traffic.

Tara gaped in amazement at the glut of bicycles parked in front of the towering cruise ships while she waited for Marcus to get her bag out of the taxi. After he slammed the door, she said, "I don't see any hotels."

"I thought you wanted a post office first," he replied.

"I do," she declared, suddenly contrite because he had remembered and she hadn't. "Which way?"

He nodded across the street. She started forward, but Marcus stopped her with his hand, tugging gently to hold her back. "Watch it. They drive on the left here, you know."

"Then what are you stopping me for?" she demanded. "If I get run over, that will solve your problem for the day, won't it?"

"Do you always enjoy being this ornery?" he asked. He couldn't recall when he had had more fun sparring with someone.

She glanced away from him in embarrassment. It wasn't her normal nature. Of the three men, Marcus was the one she wanted to know best, but he also seemed to be the one who could make her angry the easiest.."Sorry," she said. "But it depends on the nature of the person I'm with. My personality can be like a mirror at times."

Once again she had managed to put him in his place. The funny thing was, he didn't mind. It was as if she had somehow glimpsed his soul, seen all of the struggles he had endured alone.

His eyes, deep blue pools in the clear light, seemed to absorb every detail of her face. He didn't answer. Tara sensed a stream of emotions bubbling beneath the surface and decided to steer clear of it. There were depths to his personality that she guessed he shared with few people. "The post office?" she reminded him as they continued to stand on Front Street, measuring each other gaze for gaze.

He picked up her bag and led the way through traffic to the other side of the street. They walked along the row of shops and boutiques facing the harbor. Tara pretended disinterest in the shop windows; any other time she would be hanging back, admiring the displays.

He tugged on her arm to make her turn up a side street away from the harbor. "The post office is a few blocks up this way," he said tersely.

Meekly, she trotted beside him. She could feel his hackles rising and decided she had better keep silent if she didn't want to introduce any more tension between them. They turned again at the corner where a cathedral caught her interest. She made a mental note to return later for a closer look at the landmark.

"Here's the post office," he announced.

"Oh, thanks," she said, stepping ahead of him through the doorway, welcoming the feel of air conditioning against her flushed skin. She went to the display in the post office, selected a postcard with a picture of one of the island's seashells and addressed a hasty note to Julie. The poetic descriptions were for Dick's benefit when he read the card later. If she had put down her actual emotions right then, the card would have read, "Bermuda. Terrible company. Makes Dick's presence seem like paradise." She chewed on the edge of her pen for a minute and finished the note with "Sunnily yours, Tara."

Thinking of Dick eased the tension that had built between her and Marcus. Dick was probably sweating his way across Texas, trying not to step on rattlesnakes between rides. Or maybe he was walking through the endless wheat fields of Kansas or lost in the wilderness of Missouri. He couldn't possibly have gotten as far as Tara, but curiosity was eating at her. She might splurge with a phone call to Julie to find out if she had heard anything from Jim about Dick's whereabouts, but she would have to be careful not to reveal how she was getting from place to place in case word got back to Dick.

She recapped her pen and looked up to see where Marcus had gone. While she had written the note, he had taken the time to stand in line for her. She handed the card to him to mail. He looked at the scene she had chosen, flipped over the back to put the stamp on and dropped it down the slot.

As they reached the exit, rain suddenly showered down. Tara smiled. What more could she ask for to go with Marcus's "sunny" disposition? Marcus shut the post office door and said, "I think we'll be more comfortable waiting in here until the rain slackens. You're not in a hurry, are you?"

She shook her head. "You're the timekeeper. I couldn't believe it when you said we were leaving at six this morning. Paul didn't even put up an argument."

"There are some areas where I outrank him. And I take advantage of it every chance I get."

Tara's eyes sparkled with interest. He was opening up to her again, admitting he played games with his boss. She wondered if he was having second thoughts about the way he had talked with her in the taxi. "You don't like George much, either, do you?"

"As a person, George is okay. I don't hold it against him that his last name is Redding. But as a pilot, that's something altogether different. He's a hindrance more than a help."

"He looks like he'd be more fun than Paul is," Tara commented, thinking of his sheepish smile when she had caught him snacking that morning.

"You'd know more about that than I would," Marcus said, reminding Tara that she was treading on thin ice again.

"Is it just because he's Marcus's cousin that he's on this trip?" she asked, no longer caring if her question sounded nosy. Marcus had already made up his mind to dislike her, so there wasn't much more damage she could do to change his opinion of her.

"He's along for much more than that."

"I know he eats a lot," Tara said, trying to be funny, "but surely he's more than ballast for the airplane."

Marcus laughed. It was the first time Tara had heard his laughter. Unlike Paul's delayed reactions, Marcus's laughter was quick and cheerful, causing her to wish he laughed more often. "George is along for a much more important reason."

"You said he wasn't helping you much as a pilot."

"That's because he's too busy worrying about all of the work Paul makes him do."

"I don't understand," Tara said, looking out the post office window to see if the rain had stopped pelting down.

"George is putting together all of the briefs for the clients while Paul does all of the fancy footwork and socializing. He's convinced that's the key to business and that he's the only man good enough for the job."

Tara frowned and thought how socializing did seem to be a priority with Paul. "What can George as a pilot know about taxes, equity and corporate tax advantages?"

"That's the point. George is an accountant first, a pilot somewhere far down the line. The type of plane we're flying, particularly as a corporate aircraft, requires a pilot and a copilot. If Paul weren't so concerned about saving money, he'd have a copilot who pulled his own weight with the work and let George concentrate on what he does best—accounting."

Tara shook her head. "Poor George."

"Poor me," Marcus corrected. "We're lucky we didn't crash into another aircraft the other day when we were off course. But that's how Paul Redding operates. He gets other people to do his work for him; then takes all of the credit."

Tara had learned that from the way Paul had made her hitchhiking contest sound as if it had been *his* idea. At least that explained Marcus's belligerence toward his employer. She wondered, though, what he still held against her.

"He treats all of his employees without consideration. I don't condone the man's ethics, either." He stared at Tara as he finished, which told her he still wasn't convinced of her innocence where Paul was concerned.

"Let me get one thing clear once and for all," she began, then lowered her voice as several islanders who were waiting for the rain to stop glanced in her direction. "If it weren't for this stupid hitchhiking contest, I wouldn't be here right now. I have no interest in Paul personally or professionally. His airplane is all that concerns me."

His eyes roamed over her face again; then he hunched his shoulder against the wall. "Maybe you'd better explain about this 'contest,'" he said. "I still don't have a clear picture of that."

He certainly hadn't heard the explanation on the yacht, Tara realized, and was suddenly glad she could tell *her* version, not Paul's.

"What's the prize?" he asked when she finished telling him the details of the contest.

She sighed. The farther along she got in this trip, the more ridiculous her motives seemed. But all it would take was one good look at Dick Shaw right now to remind her of the necessity for victory. "Satisfaction in beating the other person." She didn't want to go into her desires to be accepted by the other students.

He folded his arms across his chest. "Who's Dick?"

"Dick? You read my card."

"Glanced at it," he admitted. "Who is he?"

Tara got the distinct impression he held his breath waiting for her answer. "He's my opponent," she replied, and saw his eyebrows rise, as if asking whether that was all that Dick was. "He's a lot like Paul Redding," she continued. "Sometimes I think they're related. Maybe that explains why winning is so important to me."

"I could understand that," he said, "but it seems like you're going to extremes over nothing. Why is it so important to beat the man?"

"Things kind of mushroomed on me. You see, the kids at school started taking bets on who would win. They're counting on me. And I—" She looked outside and mumbled to make what she was saying sound less important. "I want to be treated like one of them. I figured I could do that if I won this thing against Dick." She didn't want to explain how it would also be a victory over the past, proving her ex-husband wrong, even if he never knew about the contest or the results.

He didn't comment, but looked outside to see how heavily the rain was falling. Again, as he had felt the evening before, he found himself softening toward her. For all of her education, she was trying to find ways to fit in with the group, as he was struggling to do. Maybe they weren't so different, after all. Was that why he felt drawn to her?

"Do we have far to go?" Tara asked to change the subject. "Should we make a mad dash for it?"

"Do you mind a sprinkle?"

Her hair had already frizzled from the humidity; the heat had caused her shirt to stick to her skin. A little rain wouldn't do much more damage. She wished she had taken the time to braid her hair that morning; it would have kept her appearance a little neater. "Not at all," she answered. "Let's go."

"Come on," he said, picking up their bags and taking her hand as if she needed help in crossing the street. "Let's see how far we get before the next downpour."

Half a block later, Marcus pulled her aside beneath the shelter of someone's private porch as another deluge of rain splashed to the streets. Tara laughed at the drip from the overhang that trickled down her back. She scooted closer against the building for protection. "I can just see myself explaining this alley-by-alley view of Bermuda. You give a unique tour, Marcus."

His eyes were watchful as he propped his shoulder against the stucco wall and smiled. His look made her aware of the confined space they shared. Although it was the rear entrance to someone's residence, she felt as if the two of them were the only ones on the island. The rain beat a steady tattoo against the tile roof as Tara's heart pounded from the feelings coursing through her.

She was intensely aware of him in a way she couldn't ever remember being with any man before, yet she knew so little about him and his background. Maybe that was why she was so eager to know more. She wanted to feel his hands on her arms, his mouth on her lips and his chest pressed against her breasts. She wanted those small, delicate hands of his to discover the skin beneath her clothes and to feel his kisses burning against her neck. She blushed and turned her back on him, concentrating on the rain. It wouldn't do to have him guessing the trend of her thoughts.

He could smell the freshness of her skin, standing so close beside her. She was watching him with those curious eyes that seemed to ask and at the same time invite—what? He couldn't quite read her signals, or was it his own refusal to see what she was offering because of her involvement with Paul? He didn't want to have anything to do with his employer's leftovers.

A thunderclap made her jump. Tara lurched against him, and instinctively he grasped her forearms, steadying her. There was strength in his hands, as she had guessed there would be, but also a calming gentleness. "That was close," she gasped. Now that he had his hands on her, she was more concerned with the disturbance Marcus had on her senses than the effects of any kind of electrical storm. Her heart pumped so wildly she felt he could probably feel it all the way to her fingernails.

"Not close enough," he murmured.

She knew he wasn't referring to the thunderclap. Tara turned her head so that she could see his face over her left shoulder. He hadn't removed his hands from her arms. His eyes were clear and blue, aware of every rasping half breath she took. She stared back, wordlessly asking if he was going to kiss her. Her eyes begged him closer. The rain beat heavier around them as they watched each other, waiting for someone to make the first move. Her face was inches from his own. Then, as if he decided the next step was his and he made up his mind what that step would be, his hands slid down her arms, caressingly, before he took his hands away and levered away from her, putting a slight space between them.

Tara felt flushed again and turned her face outward toward the rain. He had known what she was thinking. She had seen the same desire that had washed over her reflected in his eyes. Why hadn't he kissed her?

Tara took an extra step away from him to emphasize that his decision not to kiss her was fine with her. She was acting like a silly first-grader around him. What had happened to her aggressive-new-woman stance? What was it about Marcus Landry that made her feel shy, vulnerable, naive? He wasn't totally immune to her, or his hands wouldn't have lingered on her arms as they had just done.

Another thunderclap sounded, more distant this time as the storm rolled away, but the rain continued just as heavily. Tara concentrated on the rain spattering and splashing on the alley pavement to avoid thinking of the tumultuous emotions stirred by the man behind her.

"I think it's beginning to slacken," he said a long while later, as if it had taken him equally long to get his emotions under control. Tara glanced over her shoulder to see the same, cool, assessing expression she usually found on his face. Had she imagined the flare of passion earlier?

"I'm game for another mad dash to the next alley," Tara said.

"We're almost at Front Street now," he said. "We'll be more sheltered walking once we get back there."

"Then let's go," she said. If she stood here much longer, he might think she enjoyed being alone with him in confined spaces. Even though that was true, she didn't want him to know it.

He led the way, setting a rapid pace to the main shopping street where the taxi driver had originally dropped them. Now Tara pretended interest in the shop windows they passed rather than give Marcus the impression that she was still affected by what had almost happened between them. It wouldn't help to have him lording it over her, running back to Paul, giving him tales of kiss and tell. Obviously, the near kiss had not left him unaffected since he kept a healthy distance from Tara as they walked, whereas earlier he had taken her hand to guide her.

"Here we are," he said, ushering her into a dark-wood-paneled hotel. Tara stepped in quietly behind him, letting him do all of the talking.

Since the room wasn't ready for occupancy, Marcus suggested they go somewhere for a drink. Tara was surprised that he didn't just dump her and her bag in the lobby and pick her up when it was time for the Redding party to fly off the island. She agreed, unable to answer her own questions of why she continued to remain in his company.

"What would you like?" Marcus asked when they had joined the crowd in a nearby pub. "They have some good English beers here, if you like beer."

"That's as good as anything," she answered, studying the decor. "Surprise me."

He laughed, the first sign of tension easing since their heated moments alone in the alley. "You shouldn't say that. I just might." His eyes challenged her, talking on another level that her body understood intuitively. Whatever had caused him to draw back in the alley would not be repeated next time.

While he was at the bar, she had a chance to observe him without his knowledge. Mentally, she found herself comparing him to the other men in the pub. Without doubt, he was one of the best-looking men there.

He turned from the bar and caught her staring. "If you're hungry, we can have lunch here," he said when he returned with the drinks.

She smiled, nodding agreeably. There was a directness in his gaze that made her feel as if no one else was in the room as far as he was concerned.

Marcus had just taken his first sip from his second glass of Guinness when their table was ready. Tara picked up her drink and followed him to the corner of the sunken level where they were seated by the waitress. She left two menus with them and walked off. Tara glanced briefly at the menu and looked up.

Marcus turned his head and caught her eyes. She had worn her reddish-blond hair loose and flowing that day. A strand of it got in her eyes. He reached up and pushed the hair out of her eyes, his hand lingering next to her cheek. As if realizing what he had done, he dropped his hand and turned away.

He makes me feel shy and helpless, Tara thought. Those emotions weren't part of her makeup, particularly helplessness. She took a deep breath to steady her racing pulse. Her eyes probed the darkness, trying to figure out what was different about this man.

"Marcus, what have you got against me?"

In the darkened room his eyes were almost navy, the gaze as strong as if they could see through to her bones. If they could, she thought he would notice her melting in the look. "Give me a chance," he answered. "I'm still looking for something."

"Do you need a reason for disliking me?"

"Yes."

Tara blinked. She couldn't ever remember having such difficulty figuring someone out. Was it she in particular or women in general whom he disliked? The waitress returned to take their order, and Tara realized she hadn't noticed anything on the menu. "What do you recommend?" Tara asked Marcus.

Marcus again gave her that look that said she shouldn't put such leading questions in his power, then ran through the menu, sounding as if he ate here frequently. She accepted his suggestion of a seafood platter and watched the activity in the room until the waitress left. When they were alone again, she leaned her elbow on the wooden tabletop and said, "Why aren't you married, Marcus?"

"Who said I wasn't?"

Visibly, she drew back. It had never entered her mind that he would be. Perhaps that explained why he had decided not to kiss her in the alley earlier. "I'm sorry," she said, stammering as disappointment flooded over her. "I didn't mean to imply that you weren't. I just somehow got the impression that you were single. Maybe it was from something Paul said." She rephrased her question as she came to terms with the upheaval of emotions his answer had caused. Why should it matter? He did his best to make her dislike him, and after this trip they would never see each other again. "How long have you been married?" She played with her drink to hide her embarrassment.

"I was married a little less than a year," he answered.

"Was?" Although hope struggled to reassert itself within her, she asked herself why she should care whether he was married or not.

"When I was in high school," he answered. Sometimes it still seemed like yesterday that he had fallen in love with the class beauty queen. He had been too young to realize appearances were all that mattered to his wife. "It seemed to be the thing to do at the time. It was a struggle to make ends meet, so I dropped out of school to work. And in the same way, divorce seemed to be the next logical step in our, umm, affair. You couldn't really call what we had a marriage." He still heard the echo of his wife's taunts about his lack of education. She had always felt that she was better than he even though she had never finished school, either, since marriage had been her only goal.

Tara had been quiet while he talked. As matter-of-fact as he sounded, she thought it had cost him a lot to reveal that much to her, a near stranger. "Any children?"

"No."

"I'm sorry," she apologized. "Is that why you didn't marry again—the hurt you must have felt from the divorce?" She could understand that, having been through the same thing herself.

"I've been too busy to get married again," he answered, keeping his reasons to himself.

"If you had really wanted to get married again, you would have found someone. You're too attractive a man to be without female companionship."

He cut his eyes in her direction and asked, "So why aren't you married? Or have you left a husband behind to gallivant halfway around the world with Paul Redding? It wouldn't be the first time it happened with him."

"I'm not married."

"Why?" He picked up her hand as if to double-check for the absence of a wedding ring. "I find it hard to believe that you're still single." Of course, as smart as she was, he wouldn't be surprised if she found it difficult to find a man more intelligent than she.

"I haven't ever found a man who wanted the same things I do."

As much as he had tried to resist, by taking his anger at himself out on her, he couldn't disguise the fact that he was attracted to her. "Are you hard to please?" he asked. His eyes locked onto hers. He wanted to believe what she had told him about not liking Paul, but he had known Paul much longer than he did her.

Tara met his look and wanted to answer honestly. "Maybe I'm becoming more particular as I get older. But it seems so simple what I'm looking for and what I'd like to have with a man."

"Tell me," he said. His eyes told her he wanted to know.

She looked at their hands, still resting comfortably together. "I want someone whom I can love and who can love me, and I'd like to have children before it's too late."

"I can't believe you would have difficulty finding a man who wanted to share that wish with you," he said softly, noticing the shimmer of tears that formed in her eyes whenever she told anyone of her deepest desire.

What was happening between them? It was like being on a first date. She wanted to linger over every look he gave her, every touch of his hand. She didn't want to forget anything he was telling her. It was like pressing each image in the scrapbook of her mind. Being with him was exciting, and it had nothing to do with the setting. They could be sitting at a crossroads in Hot Coffee, Mississippi, for all of the attention she paid to their surroundings whenever he looked at her. "I've decided to name you 'the eyes'" she told him. The waitress interrupted them as she brought salads to the table.

"The eyes," he said after the waitress left them. "Has it been that bad?"

"Every time I look around, you're glaring at me like a dead fish."

"Am I the dead fish, or are you?" he asked, chuckling.

"Sometimes it's hard to tell."

His eyebrows rose, and he cocked his head in another direct stare. "It's because I haven't figured you out."

"And I haven't pegged you, either," she admitted. She shook her head and looked down. He was giving her another of those looks that made her feel shy while a chord of desire hummed through her veins. She pushed her hair behind her ears and gave him one of her own measure-for-measure stares. "Marcus, on the way here—" she began, hesitating.

As the pause drew out, he encouraged her with one word. "Yes?"

She looked up again, knowing that his eyes had not left hers. "Why didn't you kiss me?"

His eyes lingered on hers even as he leaned within kissing distance. Tara could almost taste his lips in anticipation. She could see the kiss forming in his eyes. He wanted it as much as she did. Her pulses raced as she held her breath, waiting, wondering if she should narrow the gap between them and lean that extra nudge forward to initiate the kiss. She could feel her palms sweating while her heart pumped so wildly she could feel it pulsing in her neck.

His smile reached his eyes, lighting his face, making it all the more desirous for her to kiss him. But he didn't come any closer as his eyes continued to consider her, all of her, holding her attention as if she were a charmed cobra. His look could almost be felt the way a surge of warmth rushed through her. If he could upset her emotions this tumultuously with a look, what would his lips do to hers?

Her lips parted, waiting.

"I didn't kiss you then," he said, his voice still low because his face was near enough to feel his breath against her lips, "because I didn't want you to remember the first kiss taking place in an alley, even if it was an alley in Bermuda."

She hadn't thought she could get any warmer, but a shaft of desire flamed within her. It was like adding fuel to an already-burning fire. His words revealed a romantic streak within him. "And now?" she said, her voice barely more than a breath as her lips parted and the tip of her tongue moistened her lower lip.

"Now?" he said, smiling devilishly because he knew he had her snared like a rabbit in a trap. His eyes caressed her face as if he were taking time to count every freckle. He sucked in one last long look before his lashes fluttered over his eyes, and he shook his head. "It's not time yet." His eyes darkened as he watched for her reaction.

Tara smiled. He had a way of seducing her with his eyes, tantalizing her with the wait. It was as if he knew the anticipation of being touched and touching him would heighten her desire for him. It would be difficult to pretend disinterest, knowing that he did intend to kiss her, but in his own time. It made her want him more, as if they had just kissed, touched, made love, and she couldn't get enough of him.

Chapter Four

Dear Julie:

I'm losing ground today. My ride's not ready to leave. Do you think I can add up footprints in Bermuda's sand beaches to increase my hitchhiking mileage? Surely Dick will have a few miles of his own logged on foot.

Tanning rapidly,
Tara

"Where are you?" Julie asked when Tara reached her by phone the next morning. Tara had been having second thoughts about flying on to England with Marcus and the Redding cousins. It was one thing to be stranded in the States where she could hitch a ride by highway if needed. But in England, finding a private pilot to escort her back to America might not be as simple. As it was, she wasn't certain it would be easy to catch a free flight out of Bermuda.

"I'm in Bermuda," Tara answered.

"What state is that in?"

"It's not in a state. It's in the Atlantic Ocean," Tara said with a laugh. There was a crackle on the line. Tara guessed there must be a tropical storm somewhere between her and Julie. "Haven't you gotten my first postcard?"

"The Atlantic Ocean!" Julie gasped. "Wow! That must have been some ride you hitchhiked. How did you manage that?"

"I'll tell you all of the details when I see you. I can't afford to run up too high a phone bill. The hotel charges are already straining my charge card. Have you heard from Jim or Dick?" Tara hoped she could get a sense of how far ahead she was at that point. Even if she lost a couple of days waiting for a free flight back home, she thought she could still win once she got back to the States. It might mean taking any kind of flight she could get, from a crop duster to a mail plane, but she would manage somehow.

"Yes!" Julie said, speaking rapidly. "Dick called from Mexico. I think he's heading for South America. But this is even better. Bermuda. We were all getting worried that he's getting ahead of you. Jim has been especially concerned."

Mentally, Tara tried to picture the map, wondering how many land miles her sea flights added up to. She would ask Marcus, who was certain to know. She frowned, thinking that Dick had gotten farther than she had expected. "Why is Jim concerned about how far I'm going? He's on Dick's side, isn't he?"

"He bet the baby's savings account that you're going to win."

"Oh, no," Tara groaned. All of the doctoral students had chipped in to give the baby a savings account, as "a nest egg for college," they had said. Jim's wife had cried over their thoughtfulness. "Why did he do that?"

"He's sure you're going to win, and they need the money. He's planning on doubling it so that they can use the extra amount to finish paying the hospital bill."

"But he's on Dick's side."

"Only because no one else would be, although Dick's surprisingly gotten his share of the bets, mainly from the male students. The students are still increasing their bets because we haven't gotten the first post-card from either of you. When we do, that'll be the cutoff point for betting. We're counting on you, Tara, to prove that a woman can be smart enough to beat Dick, somehow." Tara suspected Julie had been having her own doubts up until the phone call.

Tara moaned. She had half hoped to learn that Dick was lost somewhere in Mississippi, traveling in circles. The expense of staying in hotels concerned her, plus her indebtedness to Paul and the pressure he might put on her because of it. But there didn't seem any way out now unless she wanted to let down her friends in Hattiesburg. As long as she had come this far, she might as well risk going all the way.

"It surely is good to hear from you," Julie said. Tara could hear the relief in her voice, not from the phone call as much as the news that Tara was holding her own in the contest. "I've been so worried that you've been attacked or shanghaied."

"No, I'm fine," Tara said, "and my virtue maintained, so far." She wasn't looking forward to another long flight with Paul. On the flight to Bermuda he had sat close to her so that he could put his arm around her or nuzzle his cheek against hers as he leaned across her to look out of the window—at clouds. The next thing she expected was for him to turn the airplane's seats into a bed. But the stirrings of emotion she felt for Marcus were even more of a threat. A few well-chosen angry words had kept Paul in his place, but Marcus touched her vulnerability. "I'd better go. I'll drop you a postcard from the next stop."

"Any idea where that's going to be?" Julie asked.

"London," Tara said as the phone line crackled again.

"London where? Ontario, Ohio—"

"England."

"Wow!"

"But if anyone asks, you don't know anything," Tara added hastily. "If Dick ever used his brain to think, he could figure out how I've been hitchhiking and manage to get ahead of me. I'd rather keep him in deepest, darkest doubt."

"My lips are sealed," Julie answered, "but it's with a big grin."

THE MINUTE SHE STEPPED out of the London taxi, Tara knew her charge cards were in for stress. The Bentleys and Rolls-Royces lined up at the corner entry of the Dorchester Hotel confirmed her suspicions. She glanced across the street at Hyde Park and wondered if bench seats on the green were free in this neighborhood.

Marcus and George carried the baggage as Tara followed Paul into the prestigious hotel. "Ah, Mr. Redding," the clerk said as they stepped up to the desk, "and the Redding party." He smiled in Tara's direction.

Tara raised her eyebrows and looked at Paul. She would set them all straight about who was paying *her* bill immediately. "Hello," she said, advancing on the desk clerk with her most efficacious smile. "I'm Tara Jefferson." She held out her hand and shook the clerk's hand once, soundly. "I need a room separate from the Redding party. What is the least expensive single that you have?"

Embarrassed, the desk clerk said, "Oh, but I thought—"

Tara continued smiling through tightly clamped teeth. She knew what he thought, what everyone thought. Life with the Redding party was complicated enough as it was. She had just endured several hours of kissy face with Paul Redding and was in no mood to be linked to him in any form, right down to adjacent signatures on the register. From the beginning Marcus had been giving her looks that said he suspected Paul's actions to be less than innocent. Only George seemed to be more interested in room service than what happened behind closed doors.

"Forgive me," the clerk apologized. "I assumed you would be in the same suite with the others."

"Tara is traveling with us," Paul intervened, "but she insists on a separate room. You'll be disappointed," he told Tara. "The Oliver Messel suite is one of the nicest in London."

"I'm certain it is," Tara said politely, "but I keep telling you how much I don't want to inconvenience you." After the near mauling he had given her on the flight here, she was more than eager to get as far from him as possible. She was also tired. If she didn't think it would be difficult to find a private pilot heading back to the States, she would abandon ship right now. Unless Dick had figured out her tactics, she should have him beat by more than double the number of miles by this point. To the clerk she asked, "Do you have something less expensive than a suite? Something near an elevator shaft, perhaps?"

"All of our rooms are of the finest quality," the clerk assured her.

"I was afraid they would be," Tara mumbled.

"Our lowest rates for a single begin at forty-nine pounds," the clerk said.

Exhausted from the long flight and still thinking in terms of U.S. dollars, Tara said, "I guess that's not too bad."

"Unfortunately," the clerk continued, "that room is occupied." He riffled through his guest register again and said, "Ah, here we have a vacancy."

"For forty-nine pounds?" Tara asked.

"No, madam," he answered. "It's a double room, for seventy-five pounds. If you would fill this out, please."

It was only for two nights, she reasoned. The pen hovered over the top of the page before she realized pounds sterling did not exactly equal U.S. greenbacks. "George," she said, consulting him.

He was admiring a French Impressionist oil painting of a bowl of fruit. He turned and responded, "What?"

"What's the exchange rate for the pound?"

When he quoted that morning's rate, her jaw dropped. She stared at the clerk as if to say, "How can you stand there and charge me so much?" The cost of two nights' lodging was more than a month's rent for the house she shared with Julie in Mississippi. For that same amount she could buy a new set of tires for her car, have the oil changed, a lube job and get it washed and waxed. Or if she was really going to splurge, she could buy two bottles of her favorite perfume and still have enough left over for a couple of bottles—at cost—of Dom Perignon champagne. But all it was going to buy here was two nights of privacy.

Tara tapped the gold pen against the registration desk and tried to look at the expense as a bargain. Considering where she was—London, England—and how inexpensively she had gotten here—zero for transportation—it was like getting a luxury room at a discount rate. She gave in. "Do you accept credit cards?"

When she finally arrived at her room, it was so small that Tara thought it might have once been the elevator shaft; but she was grateful to collapse on the bed. Later, a shower did wonders for her spirit as she reminded herself where she was. If only she had known two months earlier that she would be vacationing in London, the pile of schoolwork wouldn't have looked so insurmountable at the time.

A knock on the door announced the sandwich she had ordered from room service. Luxury, she thought, smiling at the sandwich on the china plate. It could be roast pheasant under glass for the way it made her feel. Dick was probably eating roast chicken tonight—if he was lucky to find one that had fallen off of a poultry truck onto the highway. She imagined him hoofing his way across Mexico.

Tara picked up the shrimp sandwich and savored the taste of fresh seafood. She would be able to get her fill of delicacies from the sea while in London. And how long had it been since she had had fresh Dover sole? Dick, on the other hand, probably wouldn't manage to get his fill of wild berries picked beside the highways. Maybe he would be lucky and find an iguana to roast on a stick.

She finished the sandwich and wished she had thought to order a diet drink to go with it. The hotel had put a glass of ice water on the tray, but she was still thirsty for the taste of a cola. She set the empty tray outside her door and returned to bed, crawling between the cool sheets. She wondered how late Marcus would burn the midnight oil in setting their course for Bergen, Norway. Once he finished that, how would he spend his free time the next day?

As tired as she was, Tara fell asleep almost immediately. But a short while later she awoke, thirsty for something other than water. She turned on the bedside lamp and considered calling room service for a soft drink. It was just after midnight. She tried to think of other things so that she could drift back to sleep, but the more she concentrated, the wider awake she became. She was too used to getting up in the middle of the night, finding Julie still studying and talking with her until three in the morning. Old habits didn't die easily even when she was several thousand miles removed in the British Isles. She felt like calling Julie again just to hear a familiar voice. They had become best friends in the past year in spite of the difference in age. Julie was the only one who understood that Tara's standoffishness wasn't because she didn't want to mingle with the other doctoral students; she just needed more time for study than they did. Tara didn't allow herself to get too involved with anyone because she knew how much energy it was going to take to reach her career goals. That was another reason why winning this hitchhiking contest was important to her—to gain their respect and friendship.

Tara decided to look for a vending machine. There was probably one by the ice machine, if she could find out where that was. She pulled on her jeans and stuffed the T-shirt she slept in into the waist. She didn't bother with shoes, since she just planned to walk down the hallway. But after checking out several floors, she hadn't found any signs of a soft drink or ice machine. She was about to give up on the craving when she noticed a couple returning to their room.

"Excuse me," Tara said, attracting their attention. "Do you know where the drink machines are?"

"Pardon?" the man asked, smiling.

"I woke up in the middle of the night with a craving for a soft drink," Tara explained with a smile. "And I can't seem to find a machine anywhere. Maybe I passed it up without seeing it. Do you know where the ice machine is located? They're usually everywhere."

The man, and now the woman, as well, continued to smile as the man answered Tara with a lengthy reply—in French.

Tara laughed when she realized the communication gap was due to language rather than inability to locate the drink machine. *"Il n'y a pas de quoi,"* Tara answered, hoping that catchall phrase meant, "forget it." For good measure, she laughed and said, *"Merci."*

A door opened behind her, and the three of them turned at the sound. Lounging in the doorway stood Paul Redding, his tie loosened and his shirt half unbuttoned. "Tara," he said, his words slurring. "I thought I recognized your voice. What's the matter?"

If she had disturbed him, there was no telling how many other guests she had awakened. She turned and smiled at the French couple who had opened their door by this time. "I was looking for a drink machine," she explained for Paul's benefit. Behind him she saw George listening from the living area of the suite. They must have just returned from dinner.

"Why don't you come in?" he suggested, losing his balance as he leaned forward to touch her. She stepped back. "We have plenty to drink, don't we, George?"

"Oh, no," she said, realizing how she was dressed. "I don't want to disturb you." At least the lighting in the hallway was dimmer than the lights in his suite. She folded her arms across her chest. "I'll just drink some water, I guess. I didn't realize it was going to be this involved to find a soda."

"Aw, come on in," he insisted, reaching for her again. "We've got plenty in the refrigerator. And if you can't find anything you like there, we can try looking somewhere else." He waggled his eyebrows suggestively.

Tara didn't think it was funny and refused to cross the threshold, braless, in her bare feet and T-shirt. Thank goodness she had pulled on her jeans.

George, who had overheard the exchange, went to the suite's compact refrigerator and removed a drink for Tara. He joined Paul at the doorway and handed her a cola. "Will this do?"

"Wonderful," Tara said. "I'm sorry I disturbed you, too. Thanks, George."

"Tara, come on," Paul said, managing to get his arm around her when he reached for her that time. "Don't be such a spoilsport."

Another door opened down the hallway, and turning at the sound, Tara saw Marcus standing in the doorway. His hair was disheveled, and his look glazed as if he, too, had been asleep. His chest and feet were bare. Tara imagined him pulling on his jeans to investigate the rumpus in the hall.

Tara glanced at her own bare feet and thought of her rumpled hair and how it must look with Paul's arm around her. Inwardly, she groaned, for Marcus probably suspected that she had spent the evening in Paul's room in spite of her efforts to make her position clear to everyone. She wriggled out of his arms. "Well, thanks for the drink," she said to Paul, lifting the can so that Marcus could see it, too. "I'm going to ask at the desk in the morning if there are any drink machines near my room. Good night." She walked down the hallway, past Marcus, wishing she could do something to remove the condemning look from his eyes.

TARA AWOKE early the next morning. She had spent half the night worrying about Marcus's opinion of her midnight wanderings. Unable to get his condescending expression out of her mind, she finally decided not to belittle herself by giving him an explanation for her innocent behavior. But to make her position clear to Paul and Marcus, Tara deliberately ignored Paul's invitation to join them at the client's English garden party.

Grateful to have a day to herself, she left the hotel, enjoying the moody English morning of gray skies with a hide-and-seek sun. She had thought of spending the day sightseeing or shopping; instead, strolling through Hyde Park, she became lulled by the quiet country scene. She stretched out on the lawn near the Long Water Serpentine lake and watched two English riders and their horses trot down Rotten Row. A dog yapped in the distance; the grass smelled freshly cut. Two ducks waddled after a little girl, with her father, as she threw breadcrumbs to them. Tara closed her eyes and fell asleep.

MARCUS COULDN'T BELIEVE his eyes when he came upon Tara lying on the bank of the lake. It looked like a scene out of a painting, something conjured up in imagination. He stood watching her for a long time, trying to understand the tumultuous feelings stirred whenever he saw her. He was still at war with himself about her, not trusting what he felt when he was with her because of what he thought when he wasn't. Even if what she said about her distaste for Paul was true, Tara Jefferson wasn't a woman who would fit easily into Marcus's world. He had nothing to offer her. One day, maybe, he would when he owned his own flight service and could be his own boss, but even then they would never meet on the same educational level. He had failed in his marriage because of that once. He might not be educated, but he was smart enough not to repeat past mistakes.

Drawn to her like a moth to a flame, Marcus stepped closer and realized she was asleep. He indulged himself in the sight of her lying relaxed in the grass and imagined walking up beside her in bed. Overcome with his own images, he sat beside her and resisted the desire to touch her. Instead, he mentally ran his hands over her lightly freckled skin, knowing instinctively how supple and silky her skin would feel. She stirred in sleep, a smile forming on her sensuous lips. He wanted to kiss her, tease her with his tongue and watch her eyes light with delight from his pleasure. Marcus plucked a wildflower and leaned over her, stroking her cheeks with the soft petals.

Tara brushed at her cheek, the smile on her lips widening. For a moment Marcus thought that she had been awake all along and had known how long he had sat next to her in pleasant silence. But when she brushed at her cheek again, he knew he was tickling her awake. He watched her eyes open, becoming aware of him. Would she resent the intrusion?

Tara sat up, looking disoriented, but it wasn't the groggy effects of a nap that confused her. It was finding Marcus sitting in the grass next to her that was a surprise. "I thought you were at Paul's garden party," she said.

"I thought you were, too." He twirled the delicate flower between his fingers, then cocked his head and glanced sideways at her.

She hugged her knees and shook her head. Then she smiled. "It sounded boring. This has been much nicer, being on my own."

"Maybe I should go away and leave you alone."

"No," she said, reaching out and touching his arm. Even as he looked down at her hand, she kept it there, wanting to draw out the contact between them after she had thought he would still be angry toward her that day. "I meant, being in Paul's company would be boring. I don't mind the company, in general."

"Oh." He gave her a half smile and hesitated as if he had something to say. Tara wondered if he had spent the night worrying about her the way she had lost sleep over him. "Then I'll stay," he said, his eyes holding hers. He couldn't think of any other place on earth he wanted to be at that moment.

Feeling shy from his look, she removed her hand, hugging her knees tighter to keep them from trembling out of nervousness. What was it about Marcus that made her feel as delicate as the wildflower he held between his fingers? Her heart lurched as their eyes met. The look between them deepened momentarily before she let her eyes skip over him, pretending she hadn't noticed the intensity of his gaze. But long afterward she still felt his eyes on her. It roused her curiosity and made her pulses race. She smiled and looked toward the water, enjoying a peaceful moment with him.

They stayed that way in companionable silence for a while; then Marcus said, "I was thinking about renting a car and driving out into the countryside for a pint in a pub. Would you like to join me for a plowman's lunch?"

She laughed. Whatever a plowman's was, if it was with Marcus, she was game. "Now that you mention it, I am hungry, but what's a plowman's?"

"It's what the man in the field traditionally eats for lunch. A little bread and butter, some cheese and chutney and perhaps a cold cut or two. Are you interested?"

Tara did her best to hide her delight. She wanted to be alone with Marcus—their time together in Bermuda had left her hungry for more of his attention—but she didn't want him to know how strongly he affected her. His own reserve had made her reluctant to make her interest clear to him. "Sounds wonderful," she said.

They drove out of London into Kent, and Marcus told her all about the "Garden of England" and how the Romans had been the first to plant orchards and vineyards in the British Isles. He explained the history of the towns they passed through, how a Saxon raiding party had come ashore near Ebbsfleet in the fifth century. A Hovercraft port was located there now, along with a replica of a Viking ship that sailed from Denmark more recently to mark the fifteen hundredth anniversary of the invasion.

"You know a lot about the history of this area," Tara commented, fascinated by his storehouse of information.

He shrugged. "It's a hobby."

His curt reply warned her not to probe further, so she silently peered out the window until they passed a house with a cone-shaped roof.

"Those are oast houses," he explained, "for drying and curing hops for beer. Haven't you noticed the hop fields in this area?"

"I wouldn't know a hop from a scotch," she replied, and turned in her seat to face him as he laughed at her quip. "Marcus, you have a real flair for history."

"It's this place," he denied. "One village slips into the next so quickly, but each has its own unique story. Like Whitstable, for instance, where we just were. Legend says Julius Caesar came looking for pearls there. When he didn't find pearls inside the shells, he decided to use the oysters for food instead. Quite often you can see oyster dredging offshore. Those oyster beds are the ones they call 'Royal Whitstable Natives.'"

"No, Marcus. It's more than just the place. It's the way you talk about it. Have you ever thought of teaching history?"

"Me?" He laughed. "Teach history?"

"Sure. Why not?"

"I can't picture me teaching anyone anything considering I dropped out of high school," he said sharply.

Caught her off guard, she didn't know what to say. It was so rare to meet someone these days who hadn't finished high school at least. Was this where the source of irritation lay—in the fact that he considered her more educated than he was? She recalled his earlier comment about her studies in psychology. He had said he would have to watch his words around her. "You'd be a wonderful teacher," she insisted, trying to bolster his ego and at the same time hide her shock but realizing she also meant it. He was too intelligent to let something like a piece of paper hold him back. "There's no reason you couldn't pass one of those high school equivalency exams and get a diploma."

"I've thought about it," he admitted.

Where was her professional cool? What could she say to make him feel it was okay not to have finished high school? She sighed and said, "Studying has been difficult for me to tackle again. It drains everything out of you. I can't say that this last year has been a bed of roses. Next year won't be much easier."

"What happens after this year?" The ease had returned to his voice. Tara assumed it was because the topic had shifted to her, away from the sensitive area of his lack of schooling.

"I'll be applying for internship."

"Just like medical doctors."

"I am working toward a doctorate," she reminded him.

"Then what?"

"That will take about a year after I finish school."

"When will that be?"

She peered closely at him, intrigued with his interest in the details of her schedule. "May. But I'd like to finish my dissertation before I take my intern position and move out of Mississippi. It's a pleasant place to live, and I'm just beginning to make my roots there with the students. With the dissertation behind me, it'll be easier to concentrate on the work at hand."

"And after that year's up?"

"I'll be able to go back into practice on my own as a full-fledged psychologist."

"Will you stay in Mississippi?"

"Most likely no," she answered. "I haven't decided where I'll apply for my internship yet. It could be anywhere in the country."

They were silent as he slowed through Canterbury, where Marcus pointed out the lofty spires of the cathedral.

"Canterbury Cathedral," she breathed as Marcus drove close enough for her to see the carved effigies on the facade. "You hear about it all of your life, but you don't give much thought to it being real."

"You've probably read Chaucer."

"Bits and pieces," she said. "It's hard to avoid the *Canterbury Tales* in English Lit."

"You should read the whole thing," he said.

Tara peered closer at him, amazed that such a subject would interest him.

"You look surprised," he said.

"Well, it isn't every day I meet a man who never finished high school yet talks more knowledgeably than the average person on just about every subject that comes up."

"You don't have to go to school to read," he defended.

That nerve again, she thought, certain now that education was the source of his sensitivity. "If you recommend *Canterbury Tales*, I'll give them another chance." She paused. "Of course, I have read *A Man for All Seasons*."

"The history of Canterbury Cathedral is much more comprehensive than the fact of Becket's martyrdom. The Black Prince is buried there. He acquired the name because he always dressed in black. 'The Ingoldsby Legends' tells the tale of the bones of a pregnant servant found walled in one of the passageways. It's supposed to be the haunted passage, although I'm sure it's only one of the ghost stories of the cathedral."

"I could see where that sort of tale would fascinate anyone," Tara interjected. "Particularly the tourists."

He edged the car into a narrow lane and said, "But the steps are what impressed me the most the first time I saw the cathedral."

"Why? What's so special about them?"

"There are sagging depressions in the stone from the thousands of pilgrims who have entered Canterbury on their knees over the centuries." They passed through Canterbury and entered the open countryside again. Marcus turned off the highway into what appeared to be the driveway to someone's home. The short drive up the hill ended in an open plaza of a village. "This is Chilham, one of the prettiest villages in Kent. I thought you might like it."

Had he chosen to take her to this village for that reason? Or did he always come here with Paul's girl-friends when Paul was busy with clients?

"I've never been here at the right time of year to see it, but they tell me jousting matches take place at Chilham Castle nearby."

"You mean, as in medieval times?" she asked, taking the hand he offered to help her out of the low car.

"Yes, complete with knights with lances on horse-back." He kept her hand in his as he turned with her to cross the square.

"Except for all of the minicars," she said, "you can almost imagine what it would have looked like a couple of hundred years ago." She let him help her over the uneven cobblestones, leaning on his arm more from desire than necessity.

"I haven't checked," he said, opening a heavy oak door, "but I'm sure we'll be able to get a plowman's here."

Tara smiled as she walked through the doorway ahead of him. Surely that was an indication that he had chosen this pub solely with her in mind. He left her sitting by a bottle-glass window while he placed their order. The room was no larger than a parlor, with personal objects of the owner decorating the walls. The room smelled of peat, often burned in the tiny fireplace, which gave the room a comfortable, homey atmosphere.

When Marcus returned, he suggested, "Taste that and tell me if you like it."

"Umm. Yes. What is it?"

"A shandy. Half beer, half lemonade."

"This is delicious," she said, taking another sip. "Why can't we have things like this in America?" She leveled her elbows along the top of the table and leaned toward him. "How do you know so much about England, Marcus?"

He shrugged, drinking Guinness. "My mother was English. Poor common working stock, like her son. She used to tell all of us boys stories about her girlhood."

"How many boys?" she asked, wondering if he would give her more information about his background than he had last time she had asked. Did his hurt stem from his feelings for his mother or his exwife?

"Four of us." He sipped his Guinness. "I was the oldest."

"I would never describe you as common working stock," she said. "You seem to have done all right for yourself." She listened to the clack of the billiards from the next room and wondered how many personal questions she could get away with before he closed up on her again. It was the psychologist's curiosity.

"I haven't done half as well as I hope to someday."

After another sip of her shandy, she smiled. "That's half of the battle, Marcus. You have the kind of determination it takes to place you anywhere you want to be. Some people never even know what that drive is."

He lifted his shoulders as if what she had said was inconsequential.

"What do you want to do?" she asked, probing for more insights into his drive and desires.

"Own my own company."

"What kind?"

"Something in aviation," he said. "Flying is what I know best. It's the kind of skill that takes more doing than book learning, although there was enough of that involved when I was earning my license." He sipped his drink. "I could make more money in the oil business," he said, "and I probably will go into that for a while. Especially if I worked overseas, in Africa. That's where the money is. That's what I'm planning to do, but oil is on the downturn at the moment. They're not hiring. I'm hoping the trend is going to change soon. It wouldn't be a bad life," he continued. "A month on, a month off. And you could choose where you wanted to live."

"Where would you like to live, Marcus? Not Texas, I gather, but England, perhaps?"

He shook his head. "I'm not sure. I've seen enough places flying for Paul. So far, no one location has made me want to put down roots." His eyes met hers and held. Home could be anywhere with a woman like Tara.

For a wild moment Tara imagined that she might have a stake in his future. She lowered her glance. His looks still made her nervous, or excited. She couldn't decide which feeling predominated, and looked up for another glimpse of him.

Slowly, their eyes measured one another, smiling, dancing, daring a caress that was almost tangible, but not quite. Tara couldn't understand why she didn't take the decision making out of his hands, reach up, pull his head down to hers and kiss him as she knew he wanted to kiss her. She could almost taste the kiss. She had made much bolder moves with other men in the past, but it was different with Marcus. She couldn't take that first step. He was the one in control, and she wanted to keep it that way. It was in his eyes, in the very set of his shoulders. Whatever he was waiting for, she knew the timing still wasn't right between them. Shyly, she lowered her eyes. For a moment she waited, wondering if he would take her chin in his palm and lift her lips to his. When he didn't, she broke the spell. "What's going on in the other room?"

He had been mesmerized by her gaze. Life would be so simple if all he had to do all day long was look at her lovely face and know that she belonged to him, body and soul. But he knew she could never be more than a dream for him. "Bar billiards, I think. I don't know much about the game," he said, leaning away from her. "Why don't we go watch while we wait for our plowman's?"

The plowman's lunches were on the table when they returned. "This is wonderful," Tara said, savoring the taste of chutney and cheese. For the first time that day she thought of Dick. What would he be dining on? How far would he have gotten in his hitchhiking? She could imagine him eating at some greasy-spoon diner, choking on exhaust fumes while worrying where his next ride would come from. She smiled and asked Marcus, "Would you remind me to mail Dick a postcard before we leave? I'd like to send one from Kent."

"Do you always date college men?" he asked, wondering just how close she was to her competitor.

She shook her head, afraid to look directly at him for fear of destroying the intimacy he had begun to reveal that afternoon. "No. Intelligence is all I require." She looked squarely at him. "Not proof of a degree."

He glanced away, and she wondered if her remark had embarrassed him. "This trip is a perfect example of that."

"How?"

"Take you and Paul, for instance," she said, tearing off a morsel of brown bread. "I prefer your company over his. It has nothing to do with education. Besides," she said, picking up her knife to spread fresh farm butter over the bread, "some fields require just as much practical knowledge as book knowledge. Take psychology, for example. It takes a lot of formal schooling for advancement. But put me in an airplane and I wouldn't know what to do."

He studied her awhile longer, then picked up her hand. Almost absentmindedly he began stroking her arm. Then, gently, he brought her hand to his lips, watching for her reaction as he kissed her hand. Abruptly, almost as if he were reciting the headlines from the *London Times*, he said, "I'd like to kiss you all over. How do you feel about that?"

Tara blushed. His statement was as good as fact. She could imagine his gentle, passionate kisses flaming her soft skin. She wanted Marcus to touch her, here and now and all over. She wanted to be so lost in loving him that she would almost forget to breathe. But she couldn't tell him that. It would show him how vulnerable she felt to what he suggested; and she didn't know if she wanted to risk falling in love with him. "I'm a little amazed," she said, her voice sounding bolder than she felt.

"Why?"

"Because you haven't even kissed me properly yet."

His eyes laughed at her, igniting her desire. The look told her that when it was time for that first kiss, it would be followed by very improper actions.

"You're tired, aren't you?" she said perceptively, noticing the dark circles under his eyes.

He nodded and cupped the back of his neck as he rolled his head around. "There's a hell of a lot of responsibility in flying through international air space. It takes me awhile to unwind." The look he cast her way said that had a lot to do with his reasons for keeping her at a distance. "Just when I do start to relax, it's time to fly somewhere else. We'll have a little more time when we get to Norway."

Impulsively, she put her hand on his neck, loving the excuse to touch him. "You feel tense," she said, wanting to run her hands across his shoulders and feel the ripple of muscles beneath her fingers.

"I wouldn't do that if I were you," he said, gently removing her hand from his shoulder.

"Why not?" she asked, curious because she had reached out without thinking. He didn't strike her as a man who didn't like to be touched.

His eyes glittered as he turned to her. "Fingernails at the back of my neck are one of my weaknesses. You don't want to answer for the consequences, do you?"

She just might dare the outcome, her eyes answered back, but only when the timing was right. And it wouldn't happen by chance if it happened at all.

It was late afternoon as they left Kent. The sky had darkened with the threat of rain. They were both in quiet moods, but as they drove past a green field where a game of soccer was in progress, Tara asked, "Do you like kids?"

"Love them. I'm very middle American when it comes to my likes and desires," he answered, taking her hand again.

"How are you middle American?" she asked, pleased to feel his hand on hers. *Keep it light or he'll realize how easily he can melt your defenses.*

"Very typically," he began. "I want an apple-pie-cooking wife, a white picket fence with a shuttered and gabled house and two point five children."

Tara warmed toward him even as she told herself to be careful. She had been fooled by men saying similar things in the past, because they were things she wanted to hear. To lighten the mood, she said, "I guess that rules me out."

"I figured it would."

She turned in her seat. "What do you mean by that?"

"You don't look like the type of woman who would want children."

A feeling of longing gutted her. "Why would you think that?"

"Look at you," he said, turning to look at her. "You're acting like a teenager with this around-the-world hitchhiking venture. There doesn't seem to be a settled bone in your body. If you wanted to have children, wouldn't you be at home right now, working on it?"

"It takes two."

"I'm well aware of that," he returned. A grin flashed on his face.

She sighed. He was right in his observation about her. She didn't have time to settle down now, and this hitchhiking contest was something a school kid would be doing. "Looks are deceiving," she said.

"How's that?"

"Obviously," she said, emulating his earlier tone, "if you were the type of man who wanted babies, you would be home right now working on it, too."

For several miles he didn't say anything. She knew what she had said was treading on dangerous ground. Finally, he glanced at her again, his eyes narrowing, his eyebrows flying as he said, "You're a pretty smart lady, aren't you?"

She grinned at the compliment.

"To return to the original question, then," he said, "if the two point five children don't rule you out of my fantasy, what does?"

She smiled, liking the idea of being his fantasy. "I've never baked an apple pie in my life. And don't say it," she warned.

"Don't say what?"

"Don't say, 'No, I guess you wouldn't have.'"

"I wasn't going to say that at all," he returned. She could see the grin trying to emerge as he spoke.

"Then what were you going to say?"

He slowed the car as they returned. "Fudging counts."

She laughed. "I can't fix fudge, either."

He cut his eyes in her direction, suppressing a smile. "In certain situations, such as the apple-pie one," he began, "fudging counts if you're not caught. Like in buying one of those frozen apple pies and slipping it past me."

"You really are old-fashioned, aren't you, Marcus?" she said, laughing.

He met her eyes directly. "Yes." He grinned, and added, "Of course, there is another alternative on the apple-pie score."

"Oh?"

He hadn't taken his eyes off her. "I could always teach you how to make one."

She raised her eyebrows at that. Somehow she thought they had gotten off the subject of apple pie. Instinctively, she knew the kitchen wasn't the only place where he would surprise her.

Chapter Five

Dear Julie:

Had to pay for a train ride today. Guess Dick won't allow me to add those miles into the sum of my hitchhiking. But it was worth it to cross the roof of Norway and reach the tip of the country's longest fjord. There's still snow!

Shivering with excitement,
Tara

Tara paid for the postcard at the desk and licked the back of the Norwegian stamp. She wondered where Dick would be mailing his card from today. She grinned. If only he could see her now!

After handing the card to the desk clerk, she decided to walk outside. It was getting late, but the light was still bright on the landscape. No one else was in the garden of the *pensjonat*. Tara understood why when she felt the chill in the air. She hugged her arms about her and decided to sit for a little while. The way the light fell on one mountainside of the Sogne Fjord, leaving the other in deep shadow, reminded her of a domino. It was like dusk and dawn all at once. A cluster of houses nestled at the edge of the fjord in the tiny village of Flåm, and brightly painted rowboats

were beached on the shore. The single road skirting the
water was little more than a track and seemed to have
been built for a handful of vehicles. Behind the three-
story *pensjonat* where they stayed, the mountains were
snowcapped, the air crisp.

Positioning her chair to face the fjord, she let the
quiet surround her. She was glad she had come. The
scenery more than made up for all of the increasingly
lecherous looks Paul had given her. On the flight to
Bergen he had told her how much closer he would like
to be with her. It was enough to make her buy an air-
line ticket to New York except for the thought of the
students back home depending on her to win this
contest.

As far as Marcus was concerned, all she knew was
the more she saw him, the more confused she felt. She
wanted to know Marcus better, but at the same time
she was afraid of getting too involved. Perhaps it was
all futile, though, because after this trip it was unlikely she would ever see him again, and a casual affair just didn't interest her. Over the years she had
counseled too many lovelorn men and women to steer
clear of hopeless situations. Yet she couldn't get out
of her mind his deep blue eyes and all of the implications they held.

There was a lot about Marcus that she admired: his
humor and gentleness, his eagle-eyed awareness and
those flashes of passion she had glimpsed in his eyes.
She wanted to know more about that passion first-
hand, but something about him brought out an un-
common shyness within Tara. He made her feel
extremely feminine, fragile, afraid to make the first
move. She couldn't explain his effect on her because

it was a new experience, but it was the reason she kept wondering what his kisses would be like.

She shivered slightly in the chill air. Who would have thought, when she had argued with Dick Shaw, that she would be sitting at the tip of the longest fjord in Norway a week later? The air smelled clean, with only the faintest hint of fish wafting with the breeze. She could almost taste the nip of snow from the mountaintops within view.

They had been in snow earlier. After landing in Bergen, they had taken the Oslo Express across the roof of Norway to Myrdal Station, changing trains to Flåm. This part of the journey couldn't be counted in her hitchhiking mileage since she had paid for the train ticket. Another expense. From the money she was spending on hotels and train tickets, it would almost have been cheaper to give Jim the money for the baby and forget the bets everyone else had made on her.

It was getting late, although a glance at the landscape wouldn't tell anyone that. It was still too bright, the sky too filled with daylight to imagine it was after nine P.M. The never-setting sun in the land of the midnight sun confused her. She might as well go in. They would be taking the morning train back to Bergen, then flying to Luxembourg.

She smiled as she turned toward the *pensjonat* where Paul and George were meeting with their client. The Redding firm had certainly collected an unusual assortment of clients. This one had oil leases in the North Sea and spent his summers managing the family-owned lodge in this remote area of Norway.

It was turning cooler. The fresh weather left her wide awake and restless. Tara decided to go inside and grab her jacket to take a walk along the shore. It might tire her enough to sleep soundly this evening. Thoughts of Marcus had kept her awake lately.

Entering the warm lodge, Tara heard voices from the basement gathering room. Others, it seemed, were as wide awake as she. It was a wonder Paul hadn't insisted she stay glued to his side after they had finished dinner with their host. Tara still couldn't see what good she did for him except to feed his ego. It was getting increasingly difficult to remain polite to avoid losing her free flight home. Luckily, his clients kept him busy whenever they were on the ground.

As Tara came out of her room, the door next to hers opened, and Marcus stepped into the hallway. He looked at her with one of those searing glances that made her feel as if an electrical charge had suddenly made her skin light up. He pulled his door shut with a click, and Tara slung her jacket over her shoulder. "Hi," she said, feeling like a teenager breathlessly waiting to be invited to the senior prom.

"Going out?" he asked.

She nodded, her lips parting, but she was at a loss for words. Why did that keep happening whenever she was around Marcus? What was it about him that made her feel as if they were two highly charged batteries waiting for a single strand of copper wire to connect them? "I'm restless," she admitted. "I thought a walk might help."

"Mind if I go with you?"

She shook her head. "I'd love company. It's beautiful outside tonight, almost like day, just a little chilly."

"Are you going to be warm enough with that thin jacket?" he asked, noticing her short-sleeved blouse.

"I have a woolen sweater I could loan you. It might be a little large, but it would be much warmer."

"Please," she said, smiling. "That would be wonderful."

She waited while he unlocked his door again and went inside, leaving the door cracked while he searched for the extra sweater. He was wearing one himself with a Nordic design. She had seen similar ones for sale in a Bergen duty-free shop at the airport. "Here," he said, returning and locking his door again. "Try this on for size."

Tara laughed as he helped her pull the sweater over her head. That lightning charge of desire zipped through her again as he pulled the long strands of her hair free of the neck of the bulky sweater. "Perfect," she said as the tail of the sweater dropped below her hips.

"Hardly," he said.

"It is as far as warmth," she amended. "And right now that's all that matters." She put her key in the lock of her own door and said over her shoulder, "Let me put this jacket back; I won't need it, after all." As he had done, she left her door cracked open as she moved into the room. Were they playing games with one another, she wondered, each leaving the door open as if daring the other to come inside? She dismissed the idea as she stepped into the hall again and found his feet planted right where she had left him. "Ready," she said, and pulled her door locked with a click.

They followed the road that led away from the railway station, skirting the mirror-calm fjord. A ewe wearing a bell around her neck trotted on the road ahead of them. The ewe's two lambs frolicked nearby.

Impulsively, Tara took Marcus's arm and smiled at him. "What a lovely lambscape."

"Ohh," he groaned. "Not ewe, too, making puns."

She laughed softly, trying not to frighten the sheep. They edged closer to the animals. Tara thought they might be family pets accustomed to such close attention, but at the last moment, the ewe climbed straight up the steep mountain slope. Her bleating lambs paced back and forth at the bottom of the cliff face before tackling the climb on their own. Marcus and Tara stood watching them until the animals had crossed to the other side out of sight.

At the point of the land, Tara rested on a large jutting rock and looked back at the village. Marcus climbed up and sat beside her. She felt calm, as if her world were complete. Putting her feet up on the rock, she hugged her knees. Her voice was soft, as if the merest whisper would disturb the tranquil scene. "I can't imagine any other place I would rather be right now."

"I agree," he said, looking at her, wondering if he would ever get tired of doing so.

They sat for a long while without speaking. Words would have been superfluous. Soon the light changed fractionally, and they began to chat idly about the landscape, but Tara knew he paid little attention to what she was saying, as she did with him. She was too aware of how close he sat beside her, how much she wanted to be closer. Could he feel the heat between them? Did he know this gnawing desire that ate at her every time she was near him? How long would he go on denying the attraction?

When he slid off the rock and held up both hands to help her down, she knew that finally the timing was right. She put her hands in his, and as soon as she touched him, she knew that it was like coming home. Looking into his eyes, she saw that same vulnerable, uncertain expression that she felt she was showing him. She had never seen such openness in a man's eyes before, a desire to give and not just take, and it made her feel bolder to know that she could have the power to move this man emotionally. As her feet touched ground, he drew her into his arms, and she went to him, willingly, eagerly.

It began as a tentative kiss, his lips barely brushing hers. It was as if he wanted to deny the kiss if she should bolt away from him. Now that he had made the first move, stirring fiery embers of passion that had long been simmering and smoking, waiting for his touch, her lips parted. She sighed, easing closer, twining her arms around his neck as she remembered his love of fingernails scratching at his hairline. Right now, all she wanted was to feel his mouth on hers, his tongue teasing the tip of her own. She could save the rest for later.

Somehow Marcus had sensed it would be this way, like an explosion of energy between the two of them. It had frightened him and made him avoid touching her for so long. But now that he was holding her in his arms, feeling her warm breath mingling with his, he knew it would have been impossible to stay away much longer. And now that it felt so right, he realized the time they had delayed had almost been a waste.

His searing kiss drew her lower lip into his, tugging and nibbling as his tongue darted forward with thrusting movements. It was as if the kiss went all the way through her, and she answered him by pressing closer, hungrily asking for more. The kiss was all at once moist and erotic, inflaming her senses. She made a slow, circling exploration of his lips, then trailed kisses across his cheek to the tip of his ear. Breathlessly, she arched closer as his mouth followed the cord of her neck. She found his pulse beating there and concentrated on that as he pushed aside the bulky sweater at her shoulders.

He needed her. He wanted her.... He loved her. There was no denying it to himself any longer. That was what scared him, because he had told himself he would never let it happen again. Yet all of his resolve was broken with her. He was made helpless by her own all-consuming response to his loving.

Tara didn't stop him as his hands slid beneath the sweater, under her blouse, warming her bare skin in a way that no woolen garment ever could. She moaned against him, clinging, because she was all at once nervous, excited and ever so breathless. This was where she wanted to be. This was why she had put up with Paul Redding. Her persistence in staying with them no longer had anything to do with the hitchhiking contest. It was Marcus Landry and the searing warmth of his embrace that had made her so intent on remaining with the group, on any excuse.

Marcus chuckled at her reaction. Why fight it any longer, he asked himself. This was where he wanted to be, in her loving arms. It was senseless to deny himself such sweetness. Maybe there could never be a future for them, but there would be no way of knowing that for certain if he held his true feelings from her and didn't give his emotions a chance to grow. His arms tightened, hugging her more fiercely. He didn't want to think of losing her just when he had found her.

Tara knew Marcus was as heated and aroused as she was. Her mouth returned to his, trying to convey feverishly the tumultuous emotions that raced out of control within her, but he drew away from her, tantalizing her more for the delay.

He caught her cheeks between his palms as his eyes met hers in the half-light. Reflected there, he saw the same fiery emotions he felt. And the love. He smiled because she seemed as afraid to admit it as he.

"You're like the Northern Lights," he said, his voice husky, barely above a whisper. "You're full of light and life. When the rest of the world is still dark and sleeping, the Northern Lights are still glowing. You do that to me. No matter how I've tried to ignore you these past few days, I couldn't. I'd try to sleep at night, and you would be in my thoughts. You're too alive to be ignored even when I'm not with you." He didn't tell her how much he had fought against this moment, knowing that once he touched her, it would be hard to ever let her go.

Tara's lips parted, enchanted with what he said. "You do that to me, too," she whispered, no longer cautious of her feelings. She wanted him and this explosion of feeling to burst into flames between them.

"Don't do that," he warned, chuckling as he brought a finger to touch the outline of her lips. "You're irresistible enough as it is."

She smiled and said, "Is that so? Then why have you done such an excellent job of resisting me these past days?"

"Because," he said, the smile leaving his lips as his eyes narrowed in seriousness, "I knew when I touched you that I wouldn't be able to stop. And I could see in your eyes that you would make me stop."

"And now?" She tantalized him, her lips hovering just beneath his own. Could she trust what he was saying? Was he just telling her what she wanted to hear? *Eyes never lie,* she told herself, probing the look that deepened the blue pools. She slid her hands down his chest where she could feel his heart racing against her palm. *He's as unsure of me as I am of him,* she thought. *That's why that first move has taken so long. We were both afraid of this moment, as much as we both wanted it.*

"Now," he said, "you're saying yes."

"Yes," she said as she brought her lips to his again. She wanted to be held and cradled in his arms, to savor the salty taste of his mouth melding with hers. She felt him shuddering against her as all of his pent-up tensions were released. He gathered her closer even as she snuggled to blend her body into his. Now that they had crossed that first line of touch, neither of them wanted to stop.

Tara discovered that she had to stand slightly on her toes in order to kiss him. This close, he was much taller than he appeared. She could taste and feel the strength that she had only guessed at before. It was like savoring chocolate, she thought, going back for more, running her lips slowly around the surface of his, tasting, exploring, gently biting, yielding her mouth to his.

"I wish now," he said, whispering slightly between kisses as his lips tickled her cheekbones and dipped to the hollow of her throat, "I hadn't waited so long."

"Umm," Tara answered, turning her face to his so that his lips could play over the delicate surface of her skin.

He turned to rest his cheek against hers, cradling her head against the palm of his hand. He turned with her to face the fjord. "But isn't this a much nicer setting than that alley in Bermuda would have been?"

"I don't think I would have noticed," she said, sighing as she tried to catch control of her rapidly beating heart. "There can't be any bad settings with you, Marcus. Besides, Bermuda would have been steamy."

He laughed and looked at her. He framed her face again with his palms. It was as if she were a rare artifact he had just unpacked and he was trying to decide the best way to treasure her. His eyes danced over her face, and a smile curved his lips. "But Norwegian nights get cold," he said. "Or so I'm told."

"Really?"

"Even during the season of the midnight sun."

Tara smiled with him. She was no longer chilled. His glance alone had warmed her, like hot brandy spreading through her veins. She quivered in his arms, as if she would break if he let her go.

"Cold?" he asked, feeling her trembling. She shook her head and buried her face against his shoulder. She couldn't explain it. It was like standing on the edge of a cliff above a deep pool of water and having a raging bull at her back. In order to save herself, she knew that she had to jump, but she was afraid to take the plunge. She wasn't sure Marcus would be there to catch her once she let go of her defenses, baring her emotions to him.

Her lower lip shuddered as she looked up at him. At the same time she knew she couldn't back down. From the way he was looking at her, she knew it would be impossible for either of them to maintain a distance between them after this.

His lips took hers again with a fierce pressure that asked for and received a response, then gave and took with equal tenderness. Tara brought her hands to his jaw, holding his mouth against hers as he tried to draw away. She wanted to stay linked with him like this forever. Her senses swam, the liquid fire spreading warmer within her. His hands became more insistent beneath the sweater. Slowly his fingers walked up each bone of her spine, tingling the skin they touched. His hands slipped around her sides and gently embraced her breasts.

Desire peaked within her at his touch. He tantalized her with tenderness, firing her senses more as she became aware of his own arousal. She could feel that geyser of emotion ready to erupt within him and imagined a little cloud of steam issuing forth from the heat of their contact. The kiss in Bermuda, had it taken place, would definitely have been steamy. But this one, now that it had happened after the long delay, was unquestionably volatile.

Marcus was the first to break away. When he did, he didn't move far. Catching her hand, he laced his fingers on top of hers and turned, walking with her toward the lodge.

Until now Tara had never known what having her heart in her throat felt like. Walking beside Marcus, stealing glances at him as they approached the lodge, made her nervous, excited. She kept trying to take deep breaths to calm her racing pulse.

Her heart thumped so wildly she was certain he must feel its surge from her hand to his. From the way he kept looking at her, she knew he felt as highly

charged as she did. Knowing that he was as much unsure of her as she was of him did nothing to relax her;
if anything, it made her feel more vulnerable. It would
be easier to resist him if he displayed an arrogant self-
confidence, the way Paul would have reacted in the
same situation. Because Marcus seemed so assailable,
it showed her that this moment was not simply a dem-
onstration of his manhood or skill with a woman. He
was not trying to impress her. Instead, he was slowly,
gently, wanting to please her.

Tara wanted to delight him. Together they were entering uncharted territory where they would have to
give and take in order to find the path of pleasure. She
was half afraid of where it would lead, but she knew
that she was going to follow the path to find out.

The reception room of the lodge seemed warmer
than Tara remembered. Even the lighting appeared
brighter. The sounds of laughter from the lounge on
the lower level were farther removed. Tara felt as if she
were walking through a surreal tunnel. The only real
thing was Marcus's hand intertwined with her own.
Wordlessly, she went with him, wanting the moment
to draw out, wishing for time to creep to a halt.

When they came to the adjacent doors of their
rooms, he halted. His look and the hesitant smile
seemed to ask for her help in deciding the next step.
Tara pulled her room key from her pocket and handed
it to him. *My place,* her look said. Now that he had
made the first move, she would meet him halfway with
encouragement of her own.

Marcus inserted the key in the lock, his hands fum-
bling with the doorknob. Tara smiled and breathed a
little easier, realizing that he was as anxious about
what would happen next as she was.

Marcus pushed the door open. Tara turned on the light switch; it created soft pools of illumination from lamps on the desk and at the bedside. The door clicked shut behind them.

They stepped fully into the room. For a long moment Marcus continued to stare at her, as if asking permission to touch her again. He pushed a strand of her honey-red hair out of her eyes, and his lips parted. "You don't know how long I've wanted to be alone with you like this."

Tara put her hand on his shoulder to steady herself; his look made her feel so light-headed. She smiled at his revelation. "I can imagine," she said. "Right from the first I've had the feeling we were both having the same kind of thoughts about each other. Maybe that's why we both fought it for so long, pretending it wasn't happening."

He nodded, running his thumb back and forth across her lower lip. His chest heaved with his breathing. "It's not an accident that we're standing here together right now."

She shook her head. "No, I wanted to be with you. But it scares me, Marcus," she admitted. It was the first time she had revealed her uncertainty to any man. In the past she had always had control over her emotions. Now, though, there was something inexplicably different about this man that caused a riot of emotion to stir within her. Her destiny lay in his hands. There was still time to back away and fight it, but she couldn't.

"What are you afraid of?" he asked. "Of me?" He smiled to think they were so alike, both of them afraid of something so wonderful, both afraid to admit it.

"I don't know," she said, frowning. "I'm afraid of the way you make me feel. It all seems new to me, as if we're on the brink of discovery."

"But we are," he said, the corner of his mouth curving in a smile as the back of his hand brushed her cheek. He slipped his other hand around the back of her neck and urged her closer. To hear that she felt unsure of herself made him feel strong enough for both of them. "You're not like anyone I've ever met before, so there are no guidelines on how we're supposed to act toward each other."

Tara steadied herself against him. "Then you feel it, too?" A glow of warmth spread over her. "But what happens next? What about tomorrow?"

Some men would have promised her everlasting devotion. Others would have given her words to build upon with hope. He could have mentioned love, which she had heard before, but he didn't. "I don't know," he answered. His eyes were cautious, waiting to see if she would run from him, half concerned that she might. "Can you tell me?" he said, turning her question around.

She shook her head, biting her lower lip. Now was the time to escape if she was going to. But she didn't want to move, not if it meant away from him.

"Tomorrow is not something that we should worry about on a night like this. There will always be tomorrows, and they'll sort themselves out one by one as they arrive. Right now, I just want to concentrate on you."

She stood on tiptoe to meet his lips with her own, clinging to him out of need and longing. As his moist kisses stoked her desire, she knew that she didn't want to be anywhere else with any other man. Tara couldn't resist digging her fingers into the back of his neck, running her nails through his hair. It felt good to be touching Marcus, feeling the contours of his head and the thickness of his hair. His hands crept beneath the sweater again. The action suddenly made her impatient to be free of the bulky material.

Tara stepped out of her shoes, away from Marcus. She tugged his sweater off over her head. He pulled his own sweater off and waited, watching her. The movement had ruffled his hair, so she reached up to smooth his sandy brown locks. He caught her hand and kissed the sensitive area of her wrist. Then, as he began slowly unbuttoning her blouse, his eyes held hers. Tara's heart pumped so wildly, she thought that he must be able to see the action. When the last button came unclasped, he began to unfasten his own shirt. Tara's eyes followed his hand as his muscular, slightly bronzed chest was revealed. When his shirt was undone to the waist, she put her mouth to his chest and kissed his firm flesh.

Marcus put his hands in her hair, tugging her closer so that their bare skin could meet beneath the loosened shirts. Deftly he unhooked her bra and swept his hand across the heated expanse of her back. "Your skin is so soft," he whispered, his mouth nibbling at the lobe of her ear as his hands cupped her shoulder blades. Tara rubbed closer, exulting in the feel of her breasts against his unyielding chest. His shoulders were warm, slightly damp. She drew away slightly and let her hands roam across the shape of his chest, down his arms, around to the finely corded muscles of his back. Then she let her fingernails follow a similar course, exploring his upper torso. His breath quickened at the increased pressure of her nails against his skin, and he chuckled as he sat on the bed, carrying her with him in his arms. "I like that," he told her.

She could feel his skin ripple beneath her fingertips. She took her hands away from him long enough to shrug out of her blouse and bra, which he had pushed off her shoulders, then shoved at the material that still hid his chest from view. His skin seemed to glow in the soft light of the lamps. Gently, Marcus pushed her against the bed and hovered above her, leaning on his elbows, which were placed on either side of her. He smiled at her.

"What?" she asked, smiling back. She felt giddy and serious all at once.

He shook his head, his eyes dancing. "Nothing," he whispered, kissing her high cheekbones. "I just enjoy looking at you."

The fire that was already burning in the pit of her stomach instantly engulfed her. It was as if someone had suddenly poured hot coffee through her system, then quickly followed it with chilled Chablis. Her breasts heaved as she caught her breath. Tickling and tantalizing, Marcus ran his hands up and down Tara's ribs. His lips parted against her shoulder, opening and closing as his mouth swirled and circled over her swelling breasts, then teased the nipples with his tongue. Tara half laughed, half moaned, at the sensations mounting within her. She twined her arms around his neck and offered first one breast then the other to his sucking, searching mouth. Marcus blew against her moist skin, then looked up as his fingers dropped to the zipper of her jeans.

Inflamed with desire, Tara impatiently slid out of her jeans. She fumbled with the fastening of Marcus's belt, then leaned on her elbows to wait for his naked flesh to join hers in a heated union from ankle to shoulder. Her toes rubbed against the shin of his leg, feeling all the more bare because of the unrestricted freedom of movement. They lay on their sides, touching, hands hungry for one another. Tara splayed her palms across his breasts, scratched at his shoulders and slid her hands down his thighs. She kissed the muscles in his arms and let her tongue dart into the sensitive area inside his elbow.

Sighing, she closed her eyes as his lips seared across her belly. She reached for him as his tongue thrust lower and caught her breath at the chain reaction of emotions rippling through her. Just when she thought that she couldn't restrain the breathless pleasure any longer, his hard, thrusting tongue surprised her. He kissed her shoulder, repeating the sweet torture with a rising and falling suspense that added a mounting height of passion. He massaged her scalp and neck, leaving her pliant and all at once eager for the complete union of her body with his. She had never felt such intensity, such need, and there was still more to come.

She dug her nails into his back and shifted her hips as his hands parted her thighs and they became one. "Oh, Marcus—" She sighed, feeling as if she were pure emotion, her body pulsing around his. She held him, loving the feel of him. She locked her legs around him, drawing him deeper, feeling his hot breath fan her neck.

He romanced her with gentle motions and soft words that Tara didn't fully comprehend. She was lost in a whirlpool of sensations, racing with him, urging him faster, then breathlessly trying to catch up. Words were lost in motions as his breathing became shallower. Spinning out of control, Tara clutched Marcus as he trembled within her. Sensations flowed into the swirling vortex of her being like tides washing ashore, receding, then surging again. Every inch of her tingled with the heat of passion as she raked her nails up and down his neck and moaned, "Marcus, oh, Marcus. Oh!" The release was pure pleasure.

He chuckled and held her tightly while he regained control over his breathing. Softly he blew at the damp hair of her neck and kissed her warm skin. Protecting her from the full effect of his weight, he shifted slightly and braced his elbows beside her. His smile conveyed tenderness and something else that caused her to drop her eyes from his glance and nuzzle her face against the curve of his neck. For the first time, Tara thought, *What if I become pregnant?* A sense of calm overcame her as she answered her own question. *It will be a love child.*

Tara looked at him, then looked away, afraid he would see her own thoughts reflected in his eyes. Then, unable to resist his eyes, she wondered if it was already too late. Had she somehow fallen in love with him?

Like a sculptor putting the finishing touches on a work of art, he began brushing his fingertips up and down her side. Tara smiled. He knew how to soothe her. She wouldn't worry about this night spent together. His hands and lips were already bringing her body to life again, blocking all rational thought.

This time both of them were breathless. It pleased her to know that she could have the same erotic effect on Marcus as he had had with her. "I think I saw all of the colors of the Northern Lights just now," Marcus said much later as he lay catching his breath. He levered onto his elbow to smile at Tara. "Are you sure you don't have some Scandinavian blood in you?"

"Right now I don't feel as if I have any blood in me," she said, laughing. "You're pretty highly charged yourself. It's like plugging into an electrical outlet at a power station."

He chuckled and kissed the creamy curve of her shoulder. "Don't get poetic on me," he warned. "You've already surprised me in enough other ways."

"Have I?" All of the glances he had given her in the past had made his touch worth waiting for. One touch from Marcus was worth a million words. Now she knew that one glance could lead to a thousand caresses. Her voice turned seductive as she slanted her eyes at him. "Have I?" she asked again.

"Don't turn those soulful eyes of yours on me," he advised. "They've haunted my days and nights for the past week. Now I know that as long as you're around, I'll probably never get any sleep."

Tara's lips parted and she moistened them. Had she, unconsciously, been sending Marcus the same kind of brooding looks he had given her? Was he telling her that she would be a hard woman to forget? Or did he simply realize all women liked to be flattered?

"Are you going to evict me?" he asked, adding, "for appearances' sake? Or may I spend the night?"

Tara couldn't imagine spending the rest of the night without him. Now that they had discovered one another, she couldn't picture herself letting him walk out of her life. But he had a life of his own, one that might not have an opening for Tara Jefferson except on holiday. While they were together, she didn't want to miss anything, even if it only meant staring at each other across a room. That alone could become quite heated.

"For appearances' sake," she said, "you can leave very early in the morning."

Chapter Six

Dear Julie:

   The sky wore a crown with the Northern Lights last evening here in the land of the midnight sun. Remind me to thank Dick. I would have missed so much if he hadn't suggested we hitchhike.

In love,

Tara

Tara was the first to reach the breakfast room the next morning. A buffet was spread on a table overlooking the fjord. Ravenous, Tara filled her plate with a sampling of everything: sardines prepared three different ways, dark bread with marmalade, boiled eggs in a cream sauce, cold cuts, potato salad, fruit salad and caramel-flavored cheese. When she glanced up and saw Marcus standing just behind Paul and George, she felt herself flush from the way he was looking at her. His eyes looked smoky blue, teasing and tempting her to remember how she had felt lying in his arms not long before. His lips curved into a smile as his glance caused her face to heat up at the memories.

"My God, Tara, are you trying to eat all three meals at once today?" Paul interrupted.

Flustered, Tara noticed how high she had heaped the food on her plate and was grateful that Paul would think she was embarrassed by the amount of food on her plate rather than by the feelings stirred by a glance from Marcus. "I've decided George has the right idea: never skip a meal, especially when you're in Scandinavia."

George smiled and advanced toward the buffet, rubbing his hands together at the sight. "Is all of this just for breakfast?"

"They knew you were coming, George," she said brightly, surprised her voice wasn't singing from happiness.

George paced around the buffet like a fatted calf at auction. "If this is only for breakfast, I can't wait to see what's for lunch." He checked his watch. "Good. I should have just enough time to finish this meal before the next one begins."

Marcus laughed as he peered over George's shoulder at the array of food, his eyes still homing back to Tara whenever the others weren't looking. "You'll upset all of the weight and balance calculations for the Grumman if you eat everything you see, George, but I can't say that I blame you with a spread like this one." He picked up a plate and began piling things on it.

"Don't worry, Marcus," George replied. "I'll throw a suitcase overboard if I have to. Just as long as it's not the one with my emergency snacks in it."

Everyone laughed except Paul, who stood back, listening to the teasing banter without joining in. Tara decided he would look best with a baked apple in his mouth and a few sprigs of parsley behind his ears. He had as much life as a roasted pig on a spit.

"I thought I might go for a short hike before the train leaves this morning." Tara said, poking at a sardine. "I wanted to be sure I didn't pass out on the trail. I guess that's why I'm so hungry." Marcus caught her eye again and grinned. Hastily she glanced at her plate. If he kept looking at her like that, everyone in the room would guess what had happened between them the previous evening.

"Some of the trails looked pretty steep from the train," Paul cautioned. "I'd be concerned about stumbling roly-poly style down the path after a big breakfast like that one."

Tara lifted her shoulders and took a deep breath to steady her nerves. She could still recall the desire that had raked through her that morning with Marcus shortly before he had slipped out of her room. "There's something about this Norwegian air that makes me hungry." She cut her eyes in Marcus's direction to catch his reaction.

It was a good thing he was still standing behind George and Paul, because he did nothing to hide his pleasure at that remark.

His hair was slightly damp from his shower. She could remember the silky feel of it between her fingers. He had on a short-sleeved polo shirt; but even with her eyes closed, she could recall the line of muscles the shirt concealed. From the raised brows and short glances he sent her way, Tara knew he was refreshing his memory with every detail he had learned about her last night, as well.

"Is this Norwegian air giving you an appetite, too?" Paul asked, staring at Marcus's collection of breakfast food.

"Something is," he replied. Tara silently thanked him for not looking in her direction. Paul had already sent her enough suspicious glances without added help from Marcus.

"Try the caramel cheese," she suggested to distract Paul before he had a chance to put two and two together. "It's the tan one on the end."

"Caramel cheese?" George said. "I think I missed that."

Paul took his plate with a sweet roll and a sliver of cheese to the chair across from Tara. As she tested the egg and cream sauce, she smiled at him. He had left the place next to her free for Marcus. He would be able to sit close to her, and she could avoid his steamy glances. As soon as Marcus sat down, she felt the pressure of his leg against her own. His hand brushing her thigh was even harder to disregard. Then Paul placed his ankle against Tara's foot and slowly moved upward. Tara choked, reaching hastily for the glass of milk. She shifted her chair to discourage both of them.

"Beautiful weather, isn't it?" Paul asked as the toe of his shoe inched toward hers and his leg caressed hers again.

"Umm," Tara answered, and tucked her feet beneath her chair. "The day is so pretty," she began, talking for distraction, "that I can't wait to get outside. Anyone care to come hiking with me?" She looked directly at Paul, knowing he had another meeting with his client before the train left.

"Unfortunately, I have to meet our host this morning," Paul said. His look told her he would love nothing better than a nice short walk followed by a long roll in the hay. His foot groped toward the leg of her chair and bumped into the toe of Marcus's shoe. Paul smiled at her.

Tara turned to Marcus. "How about you? Want to come along and protect me from the mountain goats?"

"Wish I could," Marcus said, eating as if that was all that interested him while his hand gently stroked her thigh. "But I have to finish putting together our flight plan so that I'll only have to firm up the final reports of weather and flight conditions when we get to Bergen."

George left the buffet table and joined them, taking the seat next to Paul. To make room for George, Paul shifted his chair. When he resumed groping beneath the table, his questing foot encountered Marcus's shoe, which at the same time was also seeking Tara. The two men glared at one another.

"I thought I would head for the waterfall the desk clerk told us about when we checked in last night." Tara took a bite of egg and hoped Marcus realized she was telling him where to look for her just in case his excuse of paperwork had been for Paul's benefit.

"You know what time the train leaves," Paul pointed out. His foot tapped against hers again, as if daring Marcus to make a claim on her.

"I'll be back in plenty of time," she said. "As long as you're still offering a plane ride, I won't miss the connection." The sardines stared back at her as she pushed her plate away, no longer hungry. With the two men caressing her foot beneath the table, she needed some fresh air. It would only have been worse, she decided, if George had made it a threesome in toe tapping. "If you'll excuse me," she said, shoving her chair back, "I'll be on my way."

She let herself out of the *pensjonat*. The air felt fresh and cold. She wished she had Marcus's sweater to warm her again, or even better, Marcus himself. As she stepped off the veranda, she felt the sunshine on her arms and knew it wouldn't be long before she would be too warm for the jacket. As she followed the directions the desk clerk had given her, she admired the deep blue of the fjord. The sun sparkled on the surface like diamonds in the clear light. She couldn't remember seeing a more beautiful landscape; but as lovely as her surroundings were, her thoughts were still on Marcus.

It was sad that they had to pretend they were barely civil toward one another with Paul and George watching every move. She wanted to throw her arms around Marcus's neck, to walk into the room with him at the same time, to tell him all of the feelings and thoughts that bubbled over within her that morning.

At the crest of the hill, Tara paused to catch her breath and looked at the village sprawled below. This was as good a place as any to wait for Marcus. She smiled at the scenery. Except for her short, disastrous marriage, she had been alone most of her adult life, so finding pleasure in solitary occupations had almost become second nature to her. But this morning there was an emptiness within her that hadn't been there before. She began to daydream about having children one day and wondered what sort of father Marcus would make. He would be tender and gentle—she knew that from the way he had made love with her the night before. Yet he could be stern and full of discipline when necessary. She had seen that side of his nature from the aircraft problem the first day he had flown into her life. She lay down in the grass, dreaming of more nights and days of lovemaking with him.

THE GAME OF FOOTSIES with Paul resumed as soon as they settled into their seats on the train. It spoiled the view for Tara, who at first huddled closer to the window, away from Paul. Marcus, still working on his reports, glared whenever he caught her watching him, or else he pretended to ignore Tara completely. Her disappointment turned into annoyance that he hadn't been able to steal a few last moments alone with her on the hiking trail. By the time they changed trains at Myrdal Station to cross the "roof of Norway," Tara was ready to cozy up to Paul's flirtations just to get a response out of Marcus.

They landed in Luxembourg City in the evening and passed through customs control in a matter of minutes. Tara was wide awake after the long flight and the effort of keeping up her guard against Paul. It was late by the time they checked into the Hotel Cravat.

Tara didn't take long to find the way to her room. Crossing to the window, she thrust the curtains aside and looked out. By craning to the left with her nose pressed up against the glass, she could barely see the ramparts in the glow from the streetlights. She could hear the occupant of the next room pacing the floor. Fiddling with the bedside radio, Tara let an hour pass as the sounds in the adjoining room quieted. *Where is Marcus?* she kept asking herself.

Eventually, she realized he wasn't coming. She tried to remember a time when she had felt lonelier but couldn't. First he had let her spend their last morning in Norway alone; now he was ignoring her in Luxembourg. She slept restlessly and felt groggy when she woke up the next morning. Thoughts of Marcus made her angry and melancholy.

As the first light of dawn filtered through the curtains, she decided to get up and explore the town—alone. She might even find her own way to the airport and try to hitch a ride with some other pilot heading back to the States. But she knew hitchhiking was going to be more difficult from Europe. And more risky. Yet how could she bear to face Marcus again as coldly as he had treated her since their night together? He was probably having second thoughts. She had to remind herself of the men she had met in the past. While women thought in terms of emotions, most men were only interested in a woman's motions. A walk would help her clear her mind about what she should do. It was going to be a beautiful day, and she promised herself she wouldn't spend it moping. As long as she was in the heart of Europe, she was going to live it up, even if that meant feeding pigeons in the square, alone.

An hour later, she joined the people on the streets hurrying to work, busy washing sidewalks and bringing the city fully to life. Just as the shopkeeper hung out his open-for-business sign, Tara entered a bakery and selected a chocolate-covered pastry hot from the oven. Window shopping along the Place d'Armes had made her hungry. She bit into the warm pastry and licked the chocolate from her lips. She paused in a small open-air café and ordered a cup of tea and wished she didn't feel so lonely.

It wasn't like her to allow the attention of one man to cause her such agony. She tried to tell herself Marcus wasn't different from others she had met. But he was. She couldn't explain how, but he had awakened a host of feelings within her that no man had touched before.

She analyzed her feelings in her best doctor-to-patient manner. She told herself she was feeling attached to Marcus because he had managed to break through her emotional defenses. But what she couldn't understand was how that had happened. Others whom she had known longer had tried. Her attitude had softened toward other men, but it had never melted the way it had with Marcus.

It was purely physical, she told herself. But as passionate as their lovemaking had been, other images crowded her mind: the way he had been looking at her as she awoke the day before and the way he had told her in quiet moments about his mother and three brothers in Pennsylvania. His values fit so many of the slots that she wished some man would be able to fill for her. He was like an impossible dream come true. But in a matter of another day or two they might never see one another again. It would take more than wishing for anything further to come of their meeting.

When she returned to the hotel, the desk clerk greeted her cheerily. Tara resisted the urge to ask which room belonged to Marcus. He hadn't bothered to look for her, so she wouldn't take the time to seek him.

Tara smiled to the maid as she stepped out of the elevator on her floor, and had to step around the cleaning implements to reach her door. The maid had just finished with her room, and everything was neatly in place.

She kicked off her shoes and put the brochures she had collected from the tourist office on the desk, then went into the bathroom to wash her hands, still sticky after eating the pastry. Just as she was shutting off the taps, she heard a knock on her door. At least she thought it was her door. The knock had sounded lightly, as if it could have come from the room next door. Thinking that the maid might have forgotten something, Tara opened the door with a smile.

"Good morning," Marcus said, grinning back.

His presence always overwhelmed her, especially when they were standing so closely together. She took a step backward, hoping that would help steady her pounding heart. "It *was* a good morning."

He stepped into the room. "Do I detect a bit of frost?"

Tara ignored the question. "Where do you think you're going?"

"I'm not going anywhere," he answered, shutting the door behind him. "I'm already here."

"I don't recall inviting you in." She folded her arms across her chest. If she hadn't done that, it would have been too easy for her to put them around Marcus.

"You're angry."

"A lot."

"Why?"

"Why not?"

He smiled and said, "I can guess."

"What makes you think you can waltz in and out of my hotel room whenever you please?"

"If I did what I pleased," he said carefully, stepping forward again so that she had to step backward to avoid touching him, "I would waltz in—as you put it—and never waltz out again."

"Like last night, I suppose?" she said. Her heart longed for him.

"Last night," he said, "Paul had the room right next to yours. My room was next to his, not halfway across the hotel and on another floor the way it was in Norway. And George was on the other side of you."

"Oh."

"And I knew that Paul was going to want to see me first thing this morning."

"And did he?"

"Right after you left," he said, and smiled as her eyebrows rose. "Don't think I miss much where you're concerned, Tara."

"Where is Paul now? And George?"

"They've left for Vianden. They couldn't understand where you'd gone. The desk clerk hadn't seen you leaving, and you didn't answer your phone. I think they wanted you to go with them."

"Why aren't you with them?"

His eyes sparkled as he said, "I knew I was going to be busy this morning."

"Oh? Doing what?"

"Shopping."

"I suppose that explains what you're doing here now," she said. She couldn't decide if she wanted him here or not.

He shook his head. "I have a good excuse for being here."

"Really? What?"

"My room's being cleaned. I thought you might not mind if I waited here, with you, while the maid's busy."

"The shops are open," she pointed out. "There's nothing to stop you from beginning your shopping now."

"I'll buy something later," he said. His eyes never left hers.

Tara's lower lip dropped; then she laughed. That might be the excuse, but it wasn't the reason he was here. Suddenly all of her anxiety from the morning and day before left her. He didn't give her a chance to question his presence any longer for he reached out and took her in his arms.

Tara yielded to his embrace. A day away from him had been too long. He blanketed her face with tiny kisses and took her cheeks between his hands. Before she could comprehend the direction of his thoughts, he lifted her off her feet and twirled her around the room. Laughing, he set her down. "My, but you're in a good mood this morning," she said, smiling. She was no longer angry but still not satisfied about his reasons for leaving her alone for so long.

He kissed her again. "It feels good just to touch you again," he said, echoing her sentiments. "It seems much longer than twenty-four hours since I could even look at you freely without the vultures watching over their shoulders."

"Paul and George, you mean?"

He nodded.

"Forgive me for saying so," Tara began, "but you do a marvelous imitation of not liking me." She put her hand to his jaw. She smiled. Touching him like that convinced her he wasn't a dream standing in front of her. "I was beginning to think—oh, I don't know what I was thinking," she said. "I didn't like what I was thinking." She spun away from him and walked to the window.

"I can't say that I blame you," he said. He joined her and pushed the curtain aside. "You have to see that for your sake there is very little I can do with Paul and George around.'' The back of his fingers ran up and down her spine as he placed his other hand at her shoulder. He kissed the back of her neck.

Tara turned to smile at him. She placed her hand over his as it rested on her shoulder. "I know you were tired last night."

"Very," he agreed. "I had half a foolhardy mind to come scratching at your door, anyway. And I would have, too, but I fell asleep with my shoes on while waiting for Paul to settle down in the room next to me."

Tara slid her arm around his waist and snuggled next to him. "I wish you had fallen asleep next to me."

Without words, they drew together. His lips were warm and moist on hers as he pulled her lower lip into his mouth, gently sucking and nibbling. Tara sighed against him. This was where she wanted to be, where she belonged. She wound her hands around his neck, and her nails began an exploration of his neck, creeping upward, ruffling his hair.

He chuckled, laying his cheek against hers, and whispered, "You know what that does to me."

"I'm beginning to learn," she said, kissing him on the earlobe and following the line of his jaw with kisses. "Would you care to give me another lesson?"

Together they helped each other undress, their clothes thrown helter-skelter across the floor and furniture of the hotel. Marcus lifted Tara off of her feet and carried her to the bed. As their mouths met in starvation for one another, a riot of trembling emotions made Tara feel as if she were on a roller coaster and the sensations were climbing toward a peak.

Marcus kissed and whispered against her skin as his lips explored the hollow of her throat and the soft swells of her breasts. Tara slipped her hands down his muscled back, memorizing the details of his spinal cord in the valley at his lower back. She cupped her hands around his flanks and brought her hand across his flat belly. She could feel the hard jut of his pelvic bones through the muscle. Kneeling beside her, Marcus's lips never left her as he kissed the hollows between each rib and mumbled about her being too thin.

"And what will you do if I gain weight?" she whispered.

He cut his eyes toward her and smiled. "There will be more of you to love that way."

Love. Tara clutched at the word. *It's just an expression,* she told herself. *He could mean anything by it.* Even if he did mean love and not a form of "like," his definition might not fit hers. But Tara felt her whole body glow from his touch. She reveled in his soft, caressing words. If love could be so easy, she wanted to love Marcus.

Her body became more expressive, speaking to his with actions she would not allow herself to put into words. She laced her fingers around his neck, tantalizing him with her fingernails as she kissed the rounded flesh of his shoulders. Inhaling the clean scent of him, she closed her eyes and pressed her cheek against his shoulder. She wanted to spend a lifetime pleasing him, knowing that he could take equally long in ensuring her delight. She scratched at his neck, increasing the pressure, and felt the quivering reaction of pleasure ripple through him.

Chuckling softly, he moved against her, slipping his hands behind her back, sliding them down to her hips and lifting her to meet his thrusting desire.

For Tara, there was a searing moment of discomfort; then, like molten silver racing through her veins, she became fused with Marcus in an untamed impatience. She clung, wrapping her silky legs around his. Breathless, she released the stops on her emotions and let the energy of Marcus's craving carry her to the brink of mindlessness.

Closer and faster they raced. Suddenly, all too quickly, Tara felt as if she were falling, hurling headlong in ecstasy as wave after tumultuous wave engulfed her. All the while Marcus still raced, as if to catch up with her. His kisses were heated across her neck and shoulder; his breathing was ragged. She felt his breath fanning her skin and his trembling release.

He nuzzled his face against her neck, kissing her ear and blowing at the damp hair at her neck. Tara chewed on her inner lower lip to stop herself from telling him, ''I love you.'' It was something she didn't think she would ever tell another man. Yet the swell of feelings she felt for Marcus prodded those words into her mind. She tried to think of something else, but the words echoed within her. She loved Marcus. Loved him! It didn't fit into her scheme of life. She had never allowed love to enter into her relationships since her divorce. Friendship, yes. Affection, sure. But never the totally giving expression of love.

Tears puddled in her eyes. She turned her face aside to hide from Marcus. She didn't want him to see her crying, because she couldn't explain the tears. Loving Marcus would mean losing a part of herself to someone else, giving up control, wouldn't it? It had taken her so long to build up her confidence and gain her independence. She had developed such a professional cool that extended into every aspect of her life. It had helped her to keep the hurts of the past behind her. She was afraid to find out what the sacrifice of loving meant. Slowly, she took deep breaths, trying to stop crying before he noticed.

Even without her speaking, he sensed something wasn't right. "Tara?"

"Umm?" she answered, and smiled with her eyes still closed. She hoped that would disguise the confusion she felt.

He moved, bracing himself on his elbows. She felt the mattress sag from the action, then he kissed her eyelids. She smiled, keeping her eyes closed. He placed his hand on each side of her face and asked, "What's wrong?"

She shook her head, unable to speak. Smiling, she touched his wrist, her defense weakened from his tenderness.

"Look at me," he whispered.

She opened her eyes and looked at him through a glaze of tears. He touched the corner of her moist eyes and again whispered, "Tell me what's wrong. Why are you crying? Did I hurt you?"

"I'm afraid," she admitted.

"Of what?"

She gave him a crooked smile. "I'm not sure. But it has everything to do with you and me." Reaching up, she touched his cheek. He kissed her hand as it brushed his lips. She had never before admitted fear to anyone, particularly a man. She couldn't understand why she had let Marcus see her vulnerability. She was afraid to admit loving him, because it meant risking not being loved in return, the way it had happened with Rick. She blinked and took a deep breath. In the little time that they had left together, she didn't want him to remember her this way. She smiled, making light of the emotions struggling within her. "I'm probably just afraid of missing lunch," she teased, "because suddenly I've become very hungry."

He laughed and nipped at her shoulder, taking her cue that the serious discussion was closed for the moment. "There's nothing to worry about as long as you're with me," he assured her. "I know this terrific place where we can get some of the best food in town."

"Really?" A languorous feeling began to overtake her as he nibbled kisses along her sensitive inner arm. "Maybe I'm not as hungry as I thought I was, after all."

He paused long enough to say, "Well, there is room service."

Chapter Seven

Dear Julie:

Another detour, this time to Reykjavik, Iceland, for a pit stop. They call the ladies room the *Snyrting* here. Do you think Dick will be impressed to learn that? I'm off to have a Black Death. It's the national drink here, but I think it would probably fit the theme of Dick's hitchhiking better than mine, don't you?

Homeward bound,

Tara

While Marcus and George refueled the plane, Tara and Paul wandered around the airport at Reykjavik, Iceland. After mailing a postcard picturing a sheep, she accepted Paul's invitation for a drink. She didn't care much for schnapps, but he ordered a Black Death for both of them. Tara had seen the black-labeled bottles in the duty-free shop and had been curious about the taste.

An Icelandair flight landed shortly after their arrival, crowding the small airport. Tara sipped the schnapps and thought how the airport seemed only slightly larger than the one she had started out from in Mississippi nearly two weeks earlier. She had never dreamed she would end up in Iceland. Smiling at Paul, who hadn't been too obnoxious that morning, she realized she had him to thank for the success of her adventure. Feeling slightly guilty because she and Marcus had done such a great job of avoiding Paul and George the last two days, Tara decided she should make an effort to be friends with Paul. Besides, half a Black Death made her feel slightly reckless.

"Paul," she said, touching his arm, "if we have time, would you help me pick out some souvenirs in the duty-free shop? I need a man's opinion for a couple of gifts."

It was the first time she had asked for his help since she had requested a ride in his plane. Flattered that she sought his judgment, he immediately launched into a rundown on the best buys. Tara felt lighthearted by the time they picked out a long-haired sheepskin rug for Julie and a snowflake Nordic sweater for Dick. She figured the least she could do was get Dick a consolation prize. She made arrangements to have the gifts shipped home and walked arm in arm with Paul back to the plane.

Tara had barely seen Marcus that morning, since he was busy piloting the plane, but that wasn't unusual. Nighttime had become their time. She was anticipating their last evening together in Washington where they could clear customs and spend a final night before flying home the following morning. Her feelings toward him were mixed. She didn't want to act like a clinging vine, demanding to know where the relationship was going. He hadn't made any promise to her or even made the effort to exchange home addresses.

They still had tonight for final goodbyes. But she found herself hoping more than she wanted to that he would give her some sign that their time together had meant more than a casual fling to him. It was just as well that Paul had talked her into having the Black Death. It made her drowsy for the last leg of the journey, and sleeping was preferable to worrying if she were in over her head in an emotional involvement with Marcus.

Marcus woke her with a kiss after they were on the ground in Washington. Groggy from sleep and the effects of jet lag combined with the Black Death, Tara struggled awake. Her disoriented look reminded him of that morning when she had awakened in his arms. He didn't know how he was going to let her go when the journey was over, but the closer they got to home, the more unrealistic their relationship looked to him. She was a highly educated lady who traveled well in the circles Paul Redding was used to. As much tenderness as they had shared the past few days, she hadn't said anything to indicate that there was anything unusual or special about their relationship. They still had that evening to look forward to sharing together, but he was already preparing himself to hear that she wouldn't be too interested in seeing him again. Now, unable to resist her, he kissed her sleepy lidded eyes, smiling against her lips as her arms went around his shoulders and she lazily pulled him closer.

"Where are we?" she asked as she became aware of her surroundings and wondered how he had managed to elude Paul long enough to steal a kiss. Unbuckling her seat belt, she glanced out the window.

"Paul's arranging ground transportation." He tore his eyes from her sultry lips and looked out the window with her. "And here comes George. The party's over." He kissed her on the nose and asked, "See you tonight?" As long as they still had another night together, he could pretend that she belonged to him.

Smiling, Tara nodded. Both of them knew the evening would be their last. While she hoped they would see one another again, it might not be for a long while. Their eyes reflected the unspoken decisions they had delayed discussing.

It was late afternoon, and Tara was still tired from the flight. She hung close to Marcus and George, not wanting to be too obvious in her attention to Marcus. Surely George had guessed that their relationship had changed from their initial tolerance of one another. Tara wondered if Marcus had said anything to him during their long hours together in the cockpit.

Paul returned to find Marcus and George still busy in the plane. Tara thought nothing of it when he told the men, "Tara and I are going ahead. Don't wait up for us." It was what they usually did.

Marcus frowned. Tara knew he liked that arrangement as little as she did, but she would see him later at the hotel in which Paul had made arrangements for them to stay. She picked up her flight bag, happy to get to the hotel ahead of Marcus so that she could shower and take a nap before dinner. She didn't plan on sleeping at all tonight.

As Paul drove, Tara drowsed, reflecting over the past two weeks and wondering what sort of adventures Dick had had. She hadn't given him much thought since she had flown to England. The transatlantic mileage had to surpass anything he could have accumulated by thumbing rides. While she had been sitting in the lap of luxury on layover days when Paul conducted his business, Dick had probably been crossing through the jungles of the tropics and living off boa constrictor, if the snake hadn't made a meal out of him first. With his scruffy beard, the jungle environment should make him feel right at home. Maybe the natives would be so delighted to find a gringo tourist in their midst that they might even prepare a special meal for him. She could picture it now, a big steaming pot of Dick Shaw stew. Tara pitied the unsuspecting cannibals. Dick was enough to give anyone indigestion.

"What are you grinning at?" Paul asked as he noticed Tara smiling.

"Hmm? Oh. Nothing." She opened her eyes and wondered how much farther it was to the hotel. They were driving through the suburbs. Tara couldn't determine whether they were heading into D.C. or away from it. "Where are we?" she asked, sitting up straighter.

"In Virginia."

"What are we doing here? I thought we were going to the hotel."

"Not a hotel tonight," he said, taking his eyes off the road long enough to smile at her.

Tara didn't like the look of his grin. It reminded her of one of the cannibals she had just been imagining. Only now, coming from Paul, the look made her feel as if she were the entree. She moved a little closer to the door and looked more carefully at the businesses lining the highway they were following.

"I know a quiet little inn I thought you'd enjoy."

"Me and who else?" she asked warily.

"You and me, of course," he said. "Alone." The smile hadn't left his face. She could imagine the cannibal asking, "Would you like a breast or a thigh?"

"What do you mean, of course," she said, her voice stronger than she felt. "There's no 'of course' where you and I are concerned, and there's definitely not going to be an 'alone.'"

"Surely you didn't think I'd oblige you with nearly two weeks of free air travel out of the goodness of my heart," he said.

"I most certainly did!"

"Be reasonable, Tara. This is the eighties. Nobody's *that* naive anymore."

"Obviously the women you're used to giving little rides to must be," Tara returned. "I made it clear to you at the beginning and throughout the journey that I wasn't giving anything in return for putting up with your offensive company and accepting a ride in your airplane."

"I'd hardly call two weeks in the capitals of Europe one ride."

"That has nothing to do with this." She felt her hand shaking. This was one of the risks of hitchhiking that Julie had warned her about weeks ago. She should have considered this more realistically, but she had been so certain she had everything under control. She hadn't realized how deviously Paul had been watching her all day. No wonder he had left her alone; he'd been saving himself for tonight. He may have even put something in her drink to make her sleep so much on the flight. She put her hand in her lap and made a fist. The last thing she needed was to let him realize how panicked she felt. She steeled herself to put on her mask of the cool professional. Keep him talk-

ing, she told herself, while you stall for time and figure out what to do. "Just because the destinations
happened to be a good distance away and the ride
several days in length doesn't mean you earned any
frequent-flyer points in my affections."

"I'm not asking for your affection."

"What, then?" *Maybe you're jumping to conclu-
sions,* she told herself. Marcus and George might turn
up at the inn right behind them. She'd look foolish if
she yelled foul play when all Paul had in mind was a
little dinner, a little champagne, a little goodbye kiss—

"A little undivided attention in bed is all I had·in
mind. You don't have to get all emotional for my
benefit." He made certain she was looking at him
when he added, "The way you did for Marcus."

Blast it all! she thought. As careful as she and Marcus had been, Paul *and* George must have realized
what was happening between them. Out of anger came
a measure of relief. George knew where they were
going. Surely he would tell Marcus and Marcus
wouldn't let Paul get away with this.

Unless he found out about it too late. From all
Marcus had told her, George might be a Redding, but
the cousins were nothing alike. George was as un-
happy with the way Paul used him as Marcus was.
Paul wouldn't have confided in George about planning to seduce Tara. If there was any help from that
quarter, it wouldn't be arriving in the nick of time with
Sky King flying to her rescue.

Face it. She had gotten herself into this by agreeing
to the hitchhiking contest with Dick. But it was no use
blaming him. He was probably in his own hot water
right now. Besides, she had gone into this sky-hopping
scheme with her eyes open—until she had gotten side-

tracked with Marcus, at least. She'd just have to use her wits with a little psychology to get herself out of this fix.

They had turned off the highway out of the suburban section and were driving along a narrow lane thick with trees and woods and very little else. Tara had no idea where they were, but from the glow to their left, she guessed that must be west with the setting sun—or else bright lights from a city's distant haze. One or the other. She never had much sense when it came to directions. The headlights of the rental car raked the trees ahead and followed the road as it turned right. Tara hadn't seen a road sign in miles. Houses had been even less evident.

"Well," she began, speaking in a steady, matter-of-fact voice, "this sexual battery case is going to be mighty easy to prove in court." Never let the patient see that he has unnerved you, she reminded herself, knowing how difficult it *would* be to prove.

"What happens between us can hardly be construed as that when both Marcus and George watched you docilely follow me to the car."

"Yes, but all I have to do is file assault charges against you and Marcus'll be a witness on my side. We had plans to meet later tonight, and he knows I'd never willingly go anywhere with you. I'll be missed, Paul. Be reasonable."

"Assault charges! You can't be serious," he said, but she noticed he didn't sound unmoved by the suggestion. "He can hardly know you well after two short weeks. After all, what more can he think when you don't turn up? After two weeks of fun and games on the road, you're ready to go looking for new action."

"He knows me well enough to know that you're going to be in big trouble," she continued, shaking her head. "What a scandal it will create in Houston. Maybe in Dallas. Who knows, maybe all of Texas by the time I'm through with you. I have my own Texas connections," she said, dropping prominent names from a recent magazine article she had read and trying to sound as if she really knew the people. "They may not be your Libbys and Hunts, but believe me, they have enough prestige to cut you off." Tara pressed her advantage. "You know how it is when word gets around. Besides, I've worked with rape victims." She tried not to let thoughts of the stories she had heard upset her now. In court it would be her word against his. She had to keep talking calmly, reasonably. Hysterics would only egg him on. "I know what will hold up in court. I've heard some pretty bad stories to make whatever you do to me sound ten times worse. Besides," she lied, "my father's a trial lawyer."

The speed of the car had been lessening since Tara had begun speaking. But was it slowing because he was having second thoughts or slowing because he was ready to make his move? Tara prayed and kept talking. "I might even be able to prove kidnapping. Let's see. We've not only crossed state lines but borders between international countries. Hmm." She put her hand on her chin as if totally oblivious of the danger she was in. "In this country that would bring the FBI into it. That would look good on your record, don't you think, Paul?" She smiled sadly at him. All the while her heart raced as she hoped she could outwit him with words. Body language was also important in power plays. She took a deep breath to steady her nerves, but it came out as a bored sigh. She had to make him think that she was in control. "What law enforcement agencies do you think we'll have to bring in from all of those countries? There must be one for each one we've been through. Let's see; how many places have we been?"

He had let her talk long enough. "After the luxurious places you've stayed these last weeks—with your name on the hotel registers, may I remind you—it could hardly be construed as kidnapping."

"True," she admitted, not wanting logic to deter her from her plan to make him think she had the upper hand. The threat of damaging his business reputation because of a sex scandal was giving him second thoughts. "But it would be my word against yours. And believe me, Paul, I haven't been killing myself with studies for the past year for nothing. I know enough about human nature to build a pretty convincing case against you. You do, after all, follow a pattern of taking beautiful young girls along on these trips with you. I'm sure it wouldn't be difficult to get a few of your previous lovers to testify against you." She knew the minute she said it she had touched a core of bad memories.

"What do you know about my private life?" he demanded.

Her heart raced. She had blundered into a good guess. She turned it to her advantage. "You're right about one thing; Marcus and I did become fairly close. If it comes down to naming names, I'm sure he'll be of enormous help. Do you always choose blondes or redheads?" Tara was jolted forward as he slammed on the brakes.

"That's it; I've had it with you," he said, facing her as sweat glazed his angry face. "All I had in mind was a little fun and games."

"It takes a willing partner for it to be fun," Tara said, cringing mentally, wondering if she could make a run for it on this isolated road without his catching up to her. If she ran, it would throw the power into his lap, showing him just how frightened she really was.

"You were willing enough with Marcus. But you've been the biggest disappointment of this entire trip for me, taking advantage of all I had to offer, waving Marcus in my face. You little ungrateful—" He reached toward her. "This is the end of the line. Out! Right here!"

Tara didn't wait for a second invitation. She scrambled out of the car without a moment's hesitation. Grateful that she had worn flat shoes with comfort, she was ready to give Paul a good run for his monkey business, but the minute she was out of the car, it moved forward with a scattering of gravel. The door slammed shut from the force of the movement. Tara stood at the edge of the road, watching the taillights disappear around the curve. He had left her stranded!

No, she thought, *think logically.* He might have wanted her to feel safe with that thought while he turned the car around and came looking for her. She leaped into the undergrowth at the side of the road, ready to run or hide or do anything necessary to keep from ever seeing Paul Redding again. And damn the man, but he had her credit cards and flight bag in his car!

Tara hid in the woods until the chiggers and mosquitoes drove her out of the trees. Then she started walking in the direction from which they had come. Every time she heard the sound of a car, she ducked out of sight, crouching in roadside gullies or seeking safety in the trees. She walked for what seemed like hours. A blister began to form on her foot, and Tara was reminded of the day she had accepted her first hitchhiking ride. She had told the couple in the station wagon that she had had a fight with her boyfriend. That was more true now than it had been then. *Never tell a lie,* she warned herself for the future. *It always comes back on you.*

The road ahead forked. Right or left? The lady or the tiger? Tara got angry as she realized she didn't even have a coin to flip to decide the outcome. That meant she didn't even have a quarter for a phone call! And who would she call if she could? An auto service when there was no car? Julie, who was back in Mississippi and couldn't do a thing to help her? Marcus?

She turned left, trudging with a determined step and half step to ease the foot with the new blister. Would Marcus be wondering where she was? Would he be worried? Or would he be angry, too, thinking that she had gone tripping off into the sunset with Paul? Paul had set her up for this. Who could say that he hadn't concocted convincing twists on his story for Marcus's and George's benefit? By now they might both be believing she was nothing more than an opportunist, interested in nothing more than winning her idiotic hitchhiking contest. Paul could be convincing—the same way Dick had been in subtly brainwashing the graduate students about Tara being antisocial, telling them she thought she was better than the rest of them. Surely in the short time they had gotten to know each other, Marcus could know better.

The more her blister hurt, the angrier Tara became. Blast Paul for cheating her of her last evening with Marcus. She hadn't even been able to tell him good-bye. He didn't even know how to reach her when she got home—if she got home. She'd probably never see him again. It was all Dick's fault for getting her into this in the first place. No, it was her fault for not re-sisting the challenge. But it was Paul's fault she was getting a crick in her side and a limp from the blister. Most of all, it was Marcus's fault for making her fall in love with him. Tears filled her eyes, blinding her. She stumbled at the side of the road and tried to re-gain control over her emotions with a logical lecture to herself before she started crying out of frustration. And Paul, damn it, had all of her makeup in his car, too!

The moon rose above the trees, lighting her way. Tara looked at it and in spite of herself couldn't halt the tears. A full moon and no Marcus to share it with. She had to get to a phone and let him know that she was all right. But where would she call? She never knew until they arrived which hotel Paul was staying at. She could call the airport and see if someone could tell her where they had gone. Even if she could get in touch with Marcus, she had burned her bridges for a free ride home with Paul. And good riddance. But she wished they had reserved their argument for a desti-nation a little closer to home.

Her stomach growled. Tara took back every un-kind thought she had had earlier about Dick foraging for berries beside the highway. If things got that des-perate, she hoped she had the sense to distinguish poison ivy from wild herbs. Right then a drink of wa-ter would be better than a glass of champagne. If she were in the desert, at least she could chop down a cactus plant—if she could figure out how—to get to the water reserves they were supposed to contain. But if you chopped open a cactus, would there be a pocket of water inside, like that of the coconuts she bought in the supermarket?

She was getting delirious from the heat and humidity and the unexpected turn of events. Her wild thoughts kept her from noticing how far she had walked and how much farther she still had to go. *I don't like hiking,* she thought. *I'm going to like hitchhiking even less.* As each step carried her deeper into the night, she knew she was going to have to do some real hitchhiking before she was home again. She had no idea where the nearest small-craft airport was, *if* there was one here. She didn't even know what state she was in but guessed it was still Virginia. Why hadn't she paid attention to where they were going? She wouldn't have let Paul take her this far out if she had been more alert.

Tara walked until she didn't think she could take another step. Then, finding a grassy patch not far from the road, she sprawled beneath a leafy oak tree. If she had passed any houses, she hadn't noticed. At the late hour, all of the lights must have been out. She could hear a dog barking in the distance. Even more distant she thought she caught the constant rhythm of highway traffic carried on the night air. But from which direction? And how far?

She pulled the shoe off of her blistered foot and lay down, intending to close her eyes for just a minute. She would wake up and find herself in London; Marcus would be smiling at her, and this would all be a bad dream. She had never met Paul Redding. Marcus was just a figment of her imagination. She would wake up and find that she had fallen asleep with a psychology book in her hand. It would be tomorrow, and there would be a major exam to take. *This is not real,* Tara thought as she drifted to sleep.

A rock was digging into her back, right below her left shoulder blade. Tara opened her eyes, wondering where she was. Hyde Park came to mind, but she didn't think this was England. She put her hands to her cheeks, remembering, and felt the scoring of the blades of grass that had provided a scratchy pillow during the night. Tara inhaled the scent of late-blooming honeysuckle and didn't feel cheered. She could already tell it was going to be a hot day, and Paul Redding had her suntan lotion.

Sitting up, she stretched and felt a million itchy places. Her clothes were rumpled, and she longed for a bath. Most of all, she wished for a toothbrush. Paul had that, too. Sitting in the damp grass, rubbing the spot where the rock had been, Tara heard the sound of a car, or a truck. Maybe it was a moped. She stood up, hopping on one foot as she hurried into her shoe. Like it or not, it was time to hike up the leg of her designer jeans and see if she could hitch a ride. She was in such a hurry to get to the road ahead of the approaching vehicle, she skidded down the low embankment and muddied her forearm and felt her silk blouse snagging on something in the process.

A milk truck slowed and came to a stop as Tara stood in the middle of the road, flagging it down. At least it was a truck and now a cow, she thought. She closed her eyes as half of her hoped the driver would stop before he ran into her. The other half hoped he would and put her out of her misery.

"Need a lift?" the young milkman asked, calling down to her from his high seat across from the open doorway.

That was the understatement of the year, Tara thought. "Yes, please," Tara said, swallowing her pride and climbing into the lumbering vehicle.

"Where to?" he asked, eyeing her curiously but too polite to ask personal questions. He looked no older than a teenager.

"Anywhere," she said, with a sigh of relief. She was on the road again and had at least had the good fortune to pick a dairy truck for a ride. Maybe he would spare a carton of milk.

"TARA, ARE YOU OKAY? I've been so worried," Julie said two days later when Tara phoned her.

"Yes," she said with a sigh. "But I've come unhitched. I refuse to get another ride."

"You were in Washington the last anyone knew. Are you really okay? Ever since Marcus called—"

"He called?" As exhausted as Tara was from the two previous days of travel in the jolting eighteen-wheeler that had taken her from Virginia into Tennessee, Alabama and then Mississippi, the news that Marcus had called lifted her spirits.

"Yes, he's called. Who is he? I'm dying to know. He was so worried and angry, and I didn't know a thing to tell him."

Tara started laughing. All of the pain of the last miles eased with the knowledge that Marcus had somehow managed to find her. Surely that meant that she was more than a vacation fling to him and that somehow they would see one another again soon. "I'll tell you all about it on the way home. Can you come get me? I refuse to ask another stranger for a free ride. I was lucky this last guy was heading close enough to the state so that I could talk him into dropping me off in Jackson."

"Sure I'll come get you. Where exactly are you?"

"At a pay phone at—I don't know. It all seemed so wonderful just to be back in Mississippi again, I didn't really notice exactly *where* I am. Just a minute and I'll find out. But how did Marcus know to call you? I didn't give him my address."

"When you didn't show up the day after you got into Washington—I'm still dying to find out how you got from Bermuda to there—anyway, he got really angry with Paul. Who is he, Tara? Your summer adventure is beginning to sound better than a Dickens novel."

"I'll explain it later, in detail. Did Paul tell him where he'd left me?"

"I'm not sure what Paul told Marcus. Marcus didn't confide in me. But whatever it was, it was enough to make Marcus think you might be in danger. He wanted to call the police and file a missing-persons report, but they told him you hadn't been missing long enough—apparently you were gone only a few hours at that point—and anyway, Marcus and George—who's *he*, Tara? It sounds as if you met enough men to fill up two empty date books."

"I'll explain, I'll explain," Tara promised, wishing Julie would get to the point. She'd get all of the details from Marcus when she saw him. Right now she wanted to know how Marcus had found her so that she could get in touch with him. About Marcus—"

"Oh, yes, well, Marcus and George were so angry about Paul going off with you and not telling anyone that they flew off and left Paul in Washington."

"You're kidding. They did!" Tara started laughing. She could just imagine the look on Paul's face. She only wished he had been stranded in the middle of nowhere the way he had left her; but at least he had been inconvenienced in finding an alternate route back to Texas. He'd probably used credit cards, she thought, and wondered if she would get her luggage back.

"Anyway, I guess it was that same day—yesterday? Gosh, it seems longer. I've been so worried. Well, he called the university and asked for you in the psychology department. And of course everyone knows all of the graduate students, so they gave him my name and our number. And that's how he called me."

"Is he going to call again? Do you know how to contact him?"

"He left his number with me. Here, it's—"

"No, no, I'll wait until I get home," Tara said. It was enough to know that he was concerned about her. That meant they had established some sort of beginning. But they still had a lot that needed to be discussed, and she didn't feel like doing it from a public phone booth when she could be in the privacy of her own house in a few hours. "How soon can you come get me?"

"How soon can you tell me exactly where this phone booth you're calling from is located in Jackson"

"That would help, wouldn't it?" Tara said, feeling as if she were already home.

Chapter Eight

"There I was with this milk-truck driver," Tara said, laughing as she told the last of her adventures to Julie on the drive from Jackson to Hattiesburg. "We must have stopped at fifty houses at least. I didn't think anybody had their milk delivered these days. Then we went back to the plant. This kid Bill knew one of the drivers of the big trucks that service the grocery stores." She hugged her stomach, thinking of hamburgers. "I lived off yogurt and cottage cheese that day. I think they keep the ice cream for themselves."

"Was he the truck driver who brought you to Mississippi?"

Tara shook her head. "We pulled into a truck stop, and between the two of us—he was so nice to talk to the drivers he knew—we found this guy who was heading across country, with the *General*," she added.

"Who's he?"

Tara laughed. "No one you'd want to date. The *General* is his truck. Thirteen gears. All the comforts of home—if you like bouncing up and down all day in the cab. Actually it wasn't so bad when we were on the highway. It was just the side roads that he had to take slower. Flying would have been quicker, but I felt like a derelict in these clothes. I figured I'd better take what I could get at that point with the truck driver."

"Wow," Julie said as they neared Hattiesburg. "I can't believe you've been all those places."

"It was a dream," Tara said, wondering where she stood with Marcus. "With nightmare proportions near the end. But now that I'm home, even that seems funny." If she ever saw Paul Redding again, however, the anger would come back full force. "Hitchhiking is so degrading."

"I can't wait until the other kids hear your stories." Julie turned the car into the driveway and turned off the ignition key. "There's no way Dick could have beat that."

"Unless he figured out my flying system. Did anyone hear from him after he called from Mexico?"

They got out of the car and went inside. "He called one other time, from Chicago. By then you would have been flying around Europe."

Tara walked through the door and stood in the cool little house that had been home the last year. How many times while she had been studying into the early-morning hours had she wished she were elsewhere? "Home," she said, and smiled.

An hour later, Tara's hair was wrapped in a bath towel, and she was wearing her favorite robe. She curled up in the most comfortable chair in the house with a hot cup of mandarin orange tea. Julie was puttering in the kitchen after serving fluffy crab-and-Monterey-Jack omelets. She had put off calling Marcus until last. There were plenty of unanswered questions there. Since she had thought she would never see him again, she had not allowed her mind to entertain that possibility during the long, jolting truck ride home. Now she knew that she couldn't put it off any longer. He was worried about her. That said something. But would he be concerned over any woman Paul Redding had left stranded in the middle of nowhere? Or was Marcus's concern more personal?

She had waited until evening to be certain he was home. Picking up the number Julie had written down, Tara dialed. As the phone rang past three rings, she wondered if he were flying Paul to another exotic location. Or perhaps he was out on a date. Or—

"Hello?" His voice was rich and husky over the phone, as if he had just awakened.

"Marcus?" She clutched the phone tighter. "I'm sorry. Did I disturb you? This is Tara."

"Tara," he said. At first she thought he might be trying to remember who she was. But it soon became clear that she had roused him from sleep and he was having difficulty separating dreams from reality. "Tara," he said again. "Are you okay? Damn but it's good to hear you. I've been pacing the floor trying to figure out what I could do to find you."

The heat of her love for him flooded her veins as she listened to the anxiety in his voice. She wanted to be with him, feeling his arms envelop her as his voice dominated her senses. "It sounds more like you've been sleeping than pacing."

"What? Oh." She could picture him running his fingers through his tousled hair. She wished she were there to smooth it into place. "I guess I must have dozed off. I haven't been sleeping very well since I got back. If I had had my way, I would have been combing the skies looking for you, but I didn't know where to start."

"Didn't Paul tell you where he'd left me?"

"Paul never tells anyone anything," he said bitterly. "Not that I gave him a chance to say much before I decked him."

"You hit Paul?"

"Sure. What did you want me to do? Pat him on the back for stealing you away from me on our last night together and then letting you go off on your own?"

"Letting me—" She gasped. "Did he tell you that?"

"He'd said you'd had an argument and were tired of traveling with us and demanded to be dropped off at a gas station."

"That's not what happened," Tara said distinctly, getting steamed as she remembered Paul's leering advances. She filled him in on the details of their ride into the Virginia countryside.

Marcus was angry. Tara could tell by the sound of his loud breathing, like a bull ready to charge. "Damn him," he grated. "I knew something was wrong when he said you wanted to be dropped off at a gas station. That's not your style."

"It's not?" She smiled. They had learned a lot about each other in a short time without saying a word. As far apart as they were, she felt closer. He understood her.

"If you were going to be dropped off anywhere, it'd be at another airport. But I also couldn't understand why you would have just flown off without saying anything to me unless—" He paused. Tara waited. "Unless," he continued, "you had just been using us and the convenience of the plane the way Paul said."

Tara was incensed. Paul Redding had a way with words, twisting them to suit his purposes. But Marcus was intelligent enough to see beyond Paul's subterfuge. "Surely you didn't believe that," she said, holding her breath, feeling betrayed that Marcus would have considered her that selfish and calculating.

"If I had believed that, I wouldn't have tried to file a missing-persons report on you or called the hospitals in Washington for fear something had happened or worried your roommate because I didn't know where you were."

Mentally, she apologized to him. She had known that already from the little Julie had told her, but it made her feel better to hear the conviction in his voice. "Were you just concerned about my welfare, Marcus, or—" She hesitated, unable to put her fears and hopes into words.

"Or what?" he prodded.

"Or was there another reason, something more," she finished lamely. When had her assertiveness deserted her? What was it about Marcus that made her unsure of herself?

"What's that supposed to mean?" he asked. "Of course I was worried about you!"

"I mean—" she began, and took a deep breath before continuing "—is there more involved than just ordinary concern for another human being? Have we started something between us, Marcus?"

"*I* thought we had," he replied. "I had to believe that, to deny the logic of Paul's explanations. But even if I hadn't been so angry, I would still have flown out of there without him. It was worth it just to see the look on his face." He chuckled. "Tara, it was classic."

Tara wished she had been there. Someone needed to bring Paul's ego down a few notches. "It must be difficult facing him now, though, after leaving him behind in D.C.''

"Not at all. When George and I flew out of there, we knew we were signing our own flying papers, so to speak. But we figured we might as well resign in style.''

Although she could almost picture the grin on his face, Tara knew he didn't think it was all that funny. "George, too? You both lost your jobs?''

"George had been just as restless as me for months. Paul dumps all the dirty work on him, then makes him pull a double load whenever we're traveling by using him as a copilot.''

"Yes, I remember you saying how George's talents were in accounting first and aviation second.''

"Or third or fourth. We knew what we were doing when we flew off without Paul. You were just the straw that broke the camel's back.''

"Well I'm happy for you if that's what you wanted," she said uncertainly, "but Marcus, what are you doing to do now?''

"Get another job," he answered, "as soon as I can find one.''

Which wouldn't be easy with his sketchy education, Tara thought. But Marcus's experience flying should speak for itself. He shouldn't have any difficulty proving his expertise there unless Paul intervened out of revenge to make certain Marcus never got another job in Texas. Tara couldn't solve his problems for him, but she was only sorry she was at the root of them.

They talked for more than an hour, with Tara filling him in on the details of her hitchhiking trek back to Mississippi. She made him laugh when she described her burly truck driver and how he had taken her under his wing and treated her like a celebrity whenever they had stopped for a meal. All of his friends had been surprised to see him with Tara, whom he had described as his little contest winner.

"He sounds like a nice guy," Marcus said. "I'd like to thank him for taking care of you."

"He was absolutely wonderful," Tara said. "He has a big family. I'm close to his oldest daughter in age. And I've got his address. I want to send him a check for all the money he spent on me, since Paul had all of my credit cards."

"He what?"

"When I got out of the car, I didn't have time to think about my bags. As far as I know, they're still in the rental car, or else Paul still has them. I guess I should start canceling my credit cards and reapplying for new ones."

"Damn him," Marcus muttered. "I'll check on it for you. I need to see him again, anyway, now that I know what really happened."

"Marcus, don't do anything rash," Tara warned. "You might need him for a reference to get another job."

"He's not worth much as a reference—as anything—as far as I'm concerned. If I can't get another job without Paul Redding's help, then I guess I'm not worth much." Tara could hear his uncertainty over the prospect of looking for another job. His attitude was noble, but she wasn't certain it would pay off in practicality when it came to the inner circles of the corporate world. In spite of his obnoxious personality, Paul Redding carried clout.

Once they had brought each other up-to-date, there was silence on the phone. Tentatively, Tara asked, "Will I see you again?"

"I don't know how soon," Marcus said. "I don't have the money to fly over there until I know there's going to be some money coming in again."

Tara thought of the credit-card charges that would be catching up with her in a month or so from Europe. What was one more bill? "Maybe I could come out there."

"That'd be great," he said, "but I wouldn't be able to entertain you in the grand style you're used to."

Tara was happy to hear the excitement in his voice at the prospect of seeing her again. It was a question of economics and fitting a few days' escape into her school schedule, which was ready to bury her in the books again. "Just being with you is a grand style, Marcus," she said, smiling at the sound of his chuckle. "I'm easily entertained, or didn't you realize that from the time we spent together?"

"How soon can you come?"

"I don't know," she said. She didn't know how she was going to arrange it and shouldn't be spending the money on more airfare right then, but somehow she would find a way. "I have to register for classes on Monday. Maybe I can arrange my schedule so that I'll be able to take some four-day weekends."

There was another silence on the line. Tara wondered if he were thinking about the gulf between their educations. It hadn't mattered before, but now that he was job hunting, he would be more aware of the inadequacies than before. Right then all that mattered was that he wanted to see her again. She would arrange it as soon as possible.

After Tara got off the phone, Julie joined her in the living room with a second cup of tea. "He wasn't the only one who's been phoning," she said after Tara had filled her roommate in on the highlights of her conversation with Marcus. "The kids at school have wanted to know when you were getting back, too."

After the last leg of the adventure, Tara's heart had softened somewhat toward Dick. She was certain she had beat him, and probably overwhelmingly, unless he had figured out her secret and taken to the air, as well. She still wanted the other students' acceptance of her into their cliques, but she wasn't certain her one-upmanship with Dick was the way to have gone about it. "After Marcus alarmed you, I hope you didn't tell them I lost my way."

"No, I was too worried about you to think too much about games. Thank goodness Marcus was staying calm about it, even if he was angry. He seemed to be doing everything possible to find you. There wasn't much to do but wait it out."

Tara draped her leg over the arm of the chair. "You didn't give it away, where I've been, did you?"

Julie shook her head. "It wasn't easy." She smiled. "I can't wait to see the look on Dick's face when he sees that postcard from Norway. And wait till we get the one from Reykjavik. He'll turn green. I hope it gets here soon." She blew across the hot tea. "I wonder what sort of postcards Dick mailed?"

"He's the only one who hasn't called," Tara said. "Maybe he thinks he's won."

"Well, let's call *him* and tell him that he hasn't."

Tara laughed at Julie's camaraderie. Every hour began to carry her back to her college ties and make the previous weeks seem more unreal. "That's too easy," Tara decided. "We need to have a quiet meeting, just the four of us—Dick and Jim and us—to compare notes."

"And postcards."

"And mileage."

"Right," Julie said. "I like it. A quiet confrontation at dawn. Like a duel. Jim and I are the seconds. But thank goodness we didn't have to go on the road and carry the torch for you like they do in the Olympics. I would have made a terrible relay."

"Why?"

"I don't even like to jog around the neighborhood, much less the world."

"I'M GLAD you're buying," Tara said as she scooted into a corner booth of Chesterfield's Restaurant opposite Dick and Jim. They had agreed beforehand that the loser would buy drinks and dinner. "My credit cards took quite a strain the last two weeks."

"Default! Default!" Dick cried, punching Jim in the ribs.

"What are you talking about?" Julie said, scooting into the booth beside Tara and setting the book she had brought with her on her lap.

"I thought we agreed to hitchhike. That means getting free rides. You weren't allowed to use credit cards."

"I didn't spend a dime on one ride," she said. She would explain and deduct the mileage on the train trip to Flåm when they got around to it. "And the last couple of days I didn't even have a dime to spend on a phone call. But there are such things as souvenirs, Dick, not to mention hotels."

"Don't mind him," Julie said, facing Tara and running her fingers lightly over the bound volume on her lap. "Dick probably didn't think about those incidentals. What did you do, Dick? Buy a newspaper and sleep on a park bench?"

He glared at Julie, but only briefly. "I bought souvenirs, too, from a foreign country at that." Tara felt a mild concern. If he didn't think he had a fighting chance, he wouldn't have let her remark pass so easily. She resisted the urge to strum her fingers against her knee.

To break the stony silence between the two factions, Jim said, "I brought a map of North America to help plot the mileage." He set the map to one side of his place setting.

Julie grinned as she took the book from her lap, set it in front of her and nonchalantly remarked, "I brought an atlas of the world."

Chapter Nine

Dear Jim:

Hitchhiking is child's play. I've discovered a way to add mileage twenty-four hours a day, and all from the comfort of a car with no driver. Let's see Tara beat this!

See ya soon, Dick

Tara and Julie sat in the booth at Chesterfield's in Hattiesburg with the atlas on their side and a pile of picture postcards that more than matched Dick's stack of cards. He had purchased cards at the post office before leaving. "I didn't want to take time looking for pretty cards on the road," he explained. "No one said you'd earn points for picturesque views." It was like playing poker, Tara thought, waiting to see the first card Jim would turn over, showing how far Dick had gotten the first day.

She and Julie leaned closer as Jim turned over a card with a New Orleans postmark. Dick's expression was as proud as if he had just found a tarot card predicting a year filled with gold and good fortune.

"Wow, Dick," Tara said. "How did you manage to get so far?"

"Easy," he said, snapping his fingers, "once I put my master plan into action." He failed to notice Julie exchange a knowing glance with Tara.

"You mean someone actually picked you up from Highway 11?"

"Where's that waiter?" Dick asked. "I'm ready for a drink."

Tara bit her cheek to refrain from smiling and waited patiently through the distraction of the waiter's taking their drink order. After the drinks arrived, Dick smiled complacently, as if the original subject had been forgotten. Tara described the kindly couple who had given her her first ride, then asked, "So what kind of ride did you start out with, Dick?"

Jim filled in the details. "A farmer with his mule took Dick as far as Petal."

"That's original," Tara said gravely.

"I realize it was a little unconventional," Dick agreed, "but nobody said *how* we could get our rides, right?"

"Right," Julie quickly agreed.

"The point is, it took me where I needed to go to catch the next ride."

"Which was—?" Tara urged him to continue.

"I hopped a freight that took me to New Orleans."

"That's fair," Julie quickly asserted, afraid to give anything away by exchanging glances with Tara.

So that had been his plan, Tara thought with relief as Jim consulted the map and estimated the distance as 150 miles. Even if he had been able to add up miles with a long-haul freight, it couldn't have equaled

Tara's mileage. "I can't imagine myself ever riding a boxcar," Tara said.

"I didn't think you would," Dick said knowingly.

"Cruise ships are more my style," she clarified. Inwardly she smiled as a worried expression briefly crossed Dick's face. To allay his suspicions, she added, "The milk truck I had to ride in was bad enough." She shuddered, remembering that morning.

"You rode in a milk truck?" Dick laughed. "You couldn't have gotten far *that* way."

"I didn't," she said. "But it was at the end of the trip and didn't matter by then. I'll tell you about it when it's my turn."

"How about you, Tara?" Dick taunted. "Let's see your first card. How far did you get the first day?"

Tara turned over the first postcard with a view of Waterside, Norfolk's festival marketplace on the harbor.

"Virginia!"

"Postmarks don't lie," Tara said. "Check the date."

It matched that on Dick's card. He glared, too annoyed to ask how she had managed to get so far in one day. In the silence, Julie opened the atlas and estimated that Tara had made 900 miles the first day.

"That's impossible," Dick sputtered.

"Maybe I was off a little," Julie admitted, trying to act serious and professional when it was all she could do not to burst with glee. "Maybe it was only 850 miles. It's hard to tell on these big maps. We'll say 850. Is that okay with you, Tara?"

"Fine." Tara lifted her glass of wine in Dick's direction. "Where did you go the second day, Dick?"

He lowered his chin like a billy goat with a grudge and defiantly turned over the second, third and fourth cards. The postmarks read Beaumont, TX, Lafayette, LA, and Houston, TX.

"Wow, all three?" Julie said as if she were impressed. "In that order? How did that happen?"

"I'll admit it wasn't one of my better days," he said. "The boxcar I got on in Norris Yard at New Orleans ended up in a mixed train to Beaumont. The train I hopped from there went back to Lafayette. I felt like a yo-yo by the time I finally made it to Houston. But that's where my luck changed."

"Oh, Dick," Julie sympathized, "you mean it got worse?"

He ignored her jeer. "The train I got on that time went down to Laredo. From there it was such a short jump into Mexico, I figured I'd take advantage of the chance to tour a foreign country." He proudly displayed another card. Tara remembered that he had called from Mexico, which had made her decide to risk the leap to London. For a minute she was back in Bermuda with Marcus, remembering how he had nearly kissed her in that sultry alley during the rainstorm. The thought of his heavy-lidded look made her ache. How long would it be before she saw him again? Tara lost track of what Dick was saying.

"Dick brought back some awfully nice presents from Mexico," Jim said, unfolding the road map so that he could figure in the extra miles. "A pretty Mexican wedding dress for my wife and a little gown for the baby."

"I figured I might as well take advantage of the exchange rate," Dick said, shrugging modestly, as if to distract them from his kindhearted nature. "And I

also figured I had a pretty good clip of miles by then."
He looked at Jim for confirmation.

"Over a thousand miles so far."

Dick described two days of sightseeing, adding a
few miles here and there with highway rides. While he
talked, Tara thought of the flight to England. Marcus
had begun to open up to her during their journey into
the countryside. A vision of his sexy eyes and his
husky voice telling her he wanted to kiss her all over
made her anxious to get home and talk to him.

"One day," Dick continued, "I was walking along
a dirt road that didn't look as if anyone had been on
it since the day of the Aztec Indians. I'm walking
along, hot and tired, wishing for a train to come
along—even though there weren't any tracks in that
part of Mexico—but I was wishing for anything at that
point. A burro would have looked good."

"Like the farmer in Petal, right?" Julie snickered.

Dick just glared and kept talking. "And I see the
dust rising in the distance."

Tara felt a moment's sympathy for him, remembering her last two days in Virginia. Because of that,
she had promised herself not to make fun of Dick no
matter how much he tried to belittle her or question
her unconventional hitchhiking methods when it came
her turn to explain.

"Are you sure you weren't lost somewhere in the
dust bowl of Oklahoma, Dick?" Julie inquired.
"Your calculations could have been all wrong."

He finished his Scotch and water. "There was no
doubt I was in Mexico," he stated, "when these two
cars drove up. Figuring this was the only chance I was
going to have at a ride, probably all day, I practically
threw myself across the road to get them to stop."

"That could have been dangerous," Tara said. But she had experienced that feeling of desperation when the milk truck had arrived the morning she had awakened beneath a tree.

"That's one of the risks of hitchhiking," Dick said gaily. He went on to describe the two cars, a Mercedes and a wreck of a Ford. The owner of both cars had just picked up his new Mercedes and was letting his servant drive the Ford home. "I got in the Ford," he explained.

"Not the Mercedes?" Julie ribbed him.

"I was lucky to be in a car," Dick answered, overlooking her sarcasm. "But not so lucky to have that driver."

"Why not?" Jim spoke up.

"There was a major language gap. Either that or the guy was deaf. I tried talking to him for several miles, but he just kept both hands on the steering wheel. We jerked along the road, sometimes going fast, sometimes going slow." He attracted the waiter's attention to bring the table another round of drinks. "Things were going along okay for a while; then off in the distance I noticed this convoy of trucks moving our way. It occurred to me that we were driving down the middle of the road, and my driver wasn't doing anything to move over. The trucks got closer, and I figured I'd better say something to the guy. He just kept both hands on the steering wheel. I noticed his knuckles getting whiter from his grip. The trucks kept moving closer. Sweat started rolling down the guy's face, and I realized *the guy didn't know how to drive*. All he knew was that the gas pedal caused the car to speed up and slow down."

"What did you do?" Tara asked, unconsciously sitting on the edge of her seat. She remembered the concern she had felt when Paul Redding's plane had first appeared in the sky above Laurel's airport and she had learned it was in trouble. But she hadn't been in as much danger at that point as Dick had been, it appeared.

"By that time I was no longer worried about what he would think of a backseat driver. The trucks were blowing their horns at us. At the last minute, I jerked the wheel away from the driver. We scraped past the first truck and screeched to a crashing halt with the second one." He settled back in his booth, savoring everyone's reaction to his story. "You've never heard such commotion caused by a Mexican accident," he said.

"I wouldn't have wanted to be there," Jim said, shaking his head. "Did anybody get hurt?"

"No, but the car and the truck were pretty banged up. And the owner was mighty *hot*. It happened around this little settlement. The crash was pretty loud, so everybody in town joined in the commotion. The drivers were arguing back and forth, and the townspeople were shaking their heads; I guess because the road was blocked. And then I noticed there was this group of kids who were sneaking into the trucks and carrying off the contents while everybody was arguing around them."

Tara laughed, picturing the scene, wondering how close to the true story Dick had stayed. Like Paul Redding, he liked to embellish the truth with interesting details. Paul had done it to explain her absence the night he had left her stranded in Virginia. Marcus still hadn't given her the full details of what he had said about her. "What did you do?" she asked Dick.

"I got out of there as soon as I could. Another car came along in the middle of the mess, and I hitched a ride with the driver." The waiter brought fresh drinks and cleared the table of the empty glasses. "But coming back into the country was where I ran into trouble."

"Which turned out to be a blessing in disguise," Jim interjected while computing the miles Dick had added in Mexico. "We're up to fourteen hundred miles in less than a week." He looked with concern at Tara. She remembered that Jim had bet the baby's savings account that she would beat Dick.

"Why don't we place our order for dinner while Dick explains what happened?" Tara suggested. At the rate they were going, they would be there half the night. She had hoped to phone Marcus before midnight to see if he had had any new leads on a job.

"But we haven't heard where you went from Norfolk, Tara," Jim said, looking worried.

"I know. But the postcards will speak for themselves," she said. "If we keep switching back and forth with our stories, we might get the mileages mixed up." If Marcus were sitting beside her, she wouldn't care if the explanations took as long as the trip itself. But he wasn't there, and she longed to hear his voice. Sitting here, listening to Dick's drawn-out tales, was keeping her from Marcus.

"Yes, but we still don't know who's going to have to pay for the bill," Dick said. "I may be in a very expensive mood tonight."

"You mean there's a shadow of doubt over who might have won this contest?" Tara challenged.

Dick considered her question and announced, "I think I'll have prime rib." He settled back with his Scotch, looking like someone who not only owned Boardwalk and Park Place but had all the hotels in the game stacked on those two Monopoly properties.

"SO THERE HE WAS, just over the border, somewhere in New Mexico," Tara said, taking up Dick's tale where he had left off as she explained it to Marcus later that night. "And he ran into a bunch of hobos, who told him what he'd been doing wrong about riding trains."

"You mean this guy Dick actually admitted he was doing something wrong?" Marcus asked, his chuckle sounding loud and close over the phone. "If that were Paul, he'd never let anyone know he'd made a mistake."

"Yes, I thought that, too," she admitted. She wanted to ask Marcus if he had had any luck in his job search, but knowing it was a sore subject with him, she found it easier to keep talking about Dick. "What he had been doing was hopping aboard any train that moved. The hobos taught him how to choose long-haul freights."

"How's that?"

"You pick a destination, and you find out what time the train leaves. Then you hop on the train that pulls out of the yard at that time." She paused. "You know how a rail yard has a multitude of tracks and a lot of trains?"

"Uh-huh. Go on."

"The hobos showed Dick where the tracks narrow down to a couple of rails at the end of the yard. They told him to wait there to catch the train that pulled out at the designated hour." She paused a minute, re-membering how triumphant Dick had looked when explaining that. "So there he was, waiting for this train that was slowly picking up speed as it left the rail yard. He could see about ten or fifteen boxcars down the line, but none of them were open." She paused for effect, as Dick had done in the telling of his story. "The train was still gathering speed. Finally, he saw an open boxcar near the end of the train and started running alongside, ready to catch it when it caught up with him." Tara felt herself running alongside him in her imagination.

"He picked a dangerous vehicle for hitchhiking," Marcus said. "Moving trains are nothing to play with."

"Yes, I know, but you have to hand it to Dick for nerve. Anyway, the train came, and went. Dick ran faster and threw his pack with the Mexican souvenirs in. He made a giant lunge for the open car and caught the door."

"Did he get in?" Marcus asked. In spite of him-self, he was caught up in the story. At least it momen-tarily made him forget his own situation.

"He hung there, trying to haul himself up into the car before he lost his grip."

"And?"

"He fell off the train."

"Was he hurt?" Marcus asked.

Tara lauhed. "Only his pride." She wished Marcus were beside her instead of hundreds of miles away. The rich sound of his laughter made her want to reach out and hug him.

"Then what happened?" Marcus prompted, thinking he should end all of his problems and become a boxcar-hopping hobo. "I guess he never saw his pack with the souvenirs again."

"Dick got those back," Tara said. "Remember, I told you the guy has nerve?"

"Don't tell me the railroad sent them to him. Did he have his return address on the presents?"

"No, he phoned the rail yard in Amarillo—that's where the train was heading—and explained the situation."

"This should be good," Marcus said. Tara could almost see his grin from the sound of his voice. "What could he possibly have dreamed up?"

"The truth," Tara said, laughing. "He explained to the stationmaster that he was a college student hitch-hiking back to school, and in trying to hop a freight, his Mexican souvenirs made it and he didn't. He described where the boxcar was on the train and where the train was coming from. The man said he didn't know what he could do about it, but he'd try to check the train when it came in. So Dick hitched a ride with a truck driver and got to Amarillo the next morning."

"This guy Dick sounds like he has nine lives," Marcus commented, thinking how much he reminded him of Paul Redding. Tara had said they were similar. Redding could take advantage of everyone in his employment and come out smelling as innocent as a daisy. He didn't give a damn about anyone but himself. "I suppose he recovered his pack." He brought his attention back to what Tara was saying.

"The stationmaster even gave Dick better advice than the hobos on how to ride the rails."

"Really?"

"He told Dick that long-distance trains have four engines on them. The engineers ride in the first two engines; the other two are empty. He told Dick to stake out the train he wanted to take and hop aboard the second or third engine— Of course, when he waved Dick on his way, he said, 'But you didn't hear that from me.'"

Marcus laughed again. "What was his mileage like at that point?"

"Low, compared to what you helped me rack up," Tara said. "Over two thousand miles. But this is where it got good."

"It couldn't have gotten as good as the way we traveled," Marcus said, that slow and seductive sound entering his voice.

"Don't distract me," Tara teased. "Don't you want to hear the rest of Dick's story?"

He laughed, because she was so easily distracted and he wanted to do more than tease her over the phone. "What did he do next?"

"He was on his way up to the engine of the train he'd decided to take to L.A. when he passed a carload of new cars. Out of curiosity he checked the cars. Three were unlocked, with keys in them. So he climbed behind the wheel of the Cadillac and rode in it across the desert on the train to L.A." Tara couldn't help laughing as she had done when Dick told his story. Marcus laughed with her. "He said he got some really strange looks as he waved at the people waiting at the railway crossings. The only thing he couldn't understand," she added, "was how just running the air conditioner and the radio could run down a car battery after only ten hours."

When he stopped laughing with her, Marcus asked, "What did his final mileage add up to?"

"He had postmarks from all over the States but the final count was around five thousand miles."

"Not good enough," Marcus said, knowing that Tara had won the contest the day she crossed the Atlantic. It seemed like such a silly thing to be doing, especially for someone with a college education; but it had brought them together. "What did he say when you told him where you'd been?"

"He tried to say it wasn't my handwriting on the postcards, that I wrote my cards before leaving town, mailed them to some foreign friends and asked them to mail them back to me."

He sounded like a poor loser, like Paul Redding, Marcus thought, but kept his opinions to himself. All he had to do was get started on the subject of Paul and Tara would realize just how frustrated he was about finding another job. Marcus was fighting an uphill battle to make his way in the job market, all because he didn't have a proper education. And here was this college man, Dick Shaw, playing hitchhiking games in the name of a "psychological study." He was as bad as Paul Redding. Both men would use their degree as a ticket through life. Experience and skill didn't seem to matter anymore.

Tara blew at her bangs. "He even accused me of staying home with the blinds closed for the past two weeks."

"I could set him straight on that," Marcus said, the hint of laughter back in his voice. It didn't take much to remember the sensuous feel of her in his arms. Without a job, his days and nights seemed doubly long. And if he wasn't thinking of work, he was thinking of Tara. Right now he didn't have anything to offer her. Without an education he might never be able to change that. He had given more serious thought to school, now that there wasn't a job to put a curve into any personal plans. But he wasn't certain if the decision to go back to school was for himself or for Tara. "Shall I come there and tell him you were with me most of the time?" He didn't know why he was suggesting it. They both knew he couldn't afford the expense right now.

"Dick's going to believe what he wants to believe. He's just a sore loser. I knew he would be." She held the phone tighter. "Do you want to see me again, Marcus?" The longer she was away from him, the more she wanted to see him again, badly. It seemed more important than ever to fly out to Texas to be with him. "You never say."

He expelled his breath. "You know I want to see you," he said. "You turned my world upside down for nearly two weeks, and when you left—thanks to Paul—you didn't even have a chance to say goodbye. You know I'd come out there if I could, but until I find a job, there's not much I can offer you."

"Is there any news?" she asked. Now that he had brought it up, it seemed safe to ask. It was difficult not to let him know how anxious she was for him to get settled into a new position.

"No," he answered curtly. "Same story. But there are plenty of more places to try. Texas is a big state." He hoped he sounded more optimistic than he felt.

"Maybe you should take a weekend off," she suggested, chewing on her lower lip as she wondered if she were making the right decision.

"That wouldn't be hard to do since every day is like being off right now."

"That's the point," she said. "You need a little diversion, something to take your mind off work for a while. I was wondering if you'd let me stay with you if I flew out there for the weekend?" She knew her question was a selfish one. She wanted to see him for herself, to find out if he felt the same way she did. It had nothing to do with taking his mind off job hunting.

The excitement in his voice told her what she wanted to hear. "Do you mean it? Can you find time to get away from your books long enough?" He didn't feel he had the right to tear her away from her studies, but if she were the one suggesting coming out, he wasn't going to stop her. He still didn't see how it could work between them, with their different backgrounds. But as long as she was willing, he wasn't ready to lose her yet.

"Yes," she said, laughing, relieved that he sounded as eager to be with her as she felt. It was one thing to tell each other what they wanted to hear on the phone; it was another thing to face each other in the flesh. "I'm planning it if it's okay with you."

"I'll camp out at the airport waiting for you," he said. "We might have to eat hamburgers and hot dogs but—"

"I just want to be with you, Marcus," she said, making her intentions perfectly clear.

Chapter Ten

Dear Marcus,
  Wish you were here or I was there. The weekend isn't arriving soon enough.

Missing you,
Tara

Marcus was standing at the airport gate when Tara emerged from the plane a week later. He caught her in his arms, lifted her off of her feet and kissed her, disregarding the number of people milling around them. "Airports are wonderful places for saying, 'Hello. I missed you,'" he said. He let her feet slip back to the floor but kept her body close against his.

"I suppose that's one of the reasons you're a pilot," she teased. "A girl in every airport?"

He framed her face with his hands and smiled before kissing her again. "Hello. I missed you."

For a long moment they stared at each other. Tara felt her heart beating, and that breathless feeling she had experienced the first time he had looked at her left her speechless. There was magic in Marcus's blue eyes that could make her forget everything, from the already-hectic schedule of studies to the concern for Marcus finding a new position. Although it was un-spoken, she could tell he wondered the same thing as she—could they have a future together? Now that they were no longer in the dreamlike environment of Eu-rope, would they even have anything in common?

In all the days they had spoken together on the phone, she had told herself she wouldn't have expec-tations where Marcus was concerned. But they both knew this weekend was more than a friendly visit. It was an opportunity for Tara to see Marcus in his own world, to learn something of his likes and habits. It was a weekend to give love a chance to blossom and grow.

Tara laughed, excited by all the possibilities the weekend held in store. She had dreamed of seeing Marcus again, of feeling his arms around her, of watching his expressions change as she rattled on about the events of her day. Looking at him wasn't enough. She threw her arms around him again and held him tightly, hiding her face against his neck. As he squeezed her closer, she felt him trembling with emotion.

After all the days and nights apart, Marcus couldn't believe she was finally here, in his arms. He inhaled the fresh floral scent of her perfume. It reminded him of the day in England when he had tickled her awake with a flower in Hyde Park. For the moment, all of his doubts about the future left him. She was here, his for the weekend. He would take one day at a time and not ask for more.

"It's so good to be with you," she whispered, hop-ing she wouldn't cry in front of him. She was a professional and had trained well to hide her emotions from clients' sad stories. But with Marcus it was hard to hide what she was feeling, even harder to keep to herself the love that was bursting inside her heart. Imagining him these past weeks was nothing compared to the solid flesh of his forearms crushing her against him. "I didn't realize how much I missed you."

He nuzzled his cheek against hers, too overcome to reply. He felt as if he were holding a dream in his arms. She was someone from another world, an educated world, higher up on the scale of society because of her intellect. If he studied from now until his final days, he could never reach her level. Yet by coming here to be with him, she had chosen to meet him on his level. He tried not to question where it would lead. Any minute now he was going to wake up and the cold light of day was going to make her disappear.

She had a million questions to ask and even more things to say. She wanted to make up for the lost evening they had missed in Washington when Paul had left her stranded. Right then she didn't think she could get enough of looking at him. The weekend ahead made her feel as if they had all the time in the world. Just for that small pocket of time she didn't want to think about books and the schoolwork that was already doubling up at home.

"Let's go claim your luggage," he said, taking her carry-on baggage in one hand and walking with his other arm around her.

"I didn't bring anything else," she said. "I figured, what good are clothes, right?"

He grinned. "Smart woman."

"But remember, I didn't have much when we went to Europe for two weeks, either."

"However, as I recall, you kept adding baggage as we went along. By the way, I have your bags." The two weeks they had spent together had been unreal, each moment together like stolen time, beginning the day he had come upon her asleep in Hyde Park. It was pure luck, or her own boredom, he had reasoned, that had led her to spend so much time with him. No matter how much she might have enjoyed herself with Marcus in Europe, he wasn't certain the same excitement between them would continue, especially when she saw his shabby apartment.

"Did you see Paul?" she asked anxiously. She kept hoping every day that he would tell her he had found a new job. She was afraid to ask too often to let him see how concerned she was for him. To be out of work could shatter anyone's self-confidence. Afraid it would blight their precious time together if she dwelled on Paul, she tried to act as if the answer was of little consequence.

Marcus's expression hardened at the mention of his ex-boss. "I ran into George; he had gotten your things back from his cousin."

Tara decided it was better to change the subject. She hugged his arm as they walked and said, "I was going to check my carry-on bag through, but I didn't have time. I was afraid I would miss my flight."

"There would have been another plane in a couple of hours."

"I know," she said, keeping stride with his rapid pace as they passed through the concourse, "but that would have given us less time together. And I would have been stuck in the waiting room of the airport on the other end. Airport lounges can be some of the loneliest places in the world. You become so anonymous in an airport."

As they strode along, he kissed her on the cheek. "I used to agree with you," he said. "But as I recall, you came out of a waiting room."

She laughed, placing her head affectionately against his shoulder. "Trust a pilot to make a pickup in an airport."

He pushed her through the exit ahead of him and directed her through the parking area. "Why did you think you would miss your flight? You were always the first one ready when we were traveling this summer."

"Traffic was heavy, for one thing."

"It's Friday. Wait until you see it here."

"Traffic wasn't all that made me late," she said, sighing and blowing at the curls on her forehead. "Classes ran late today. And I had arranged to interview a girl for my dissertation. I became so interested in what she was telling me, I kept asking questions. That kept her talking well past the hour I had allowed for the interview. Anyway, I kept thinking I would make up for lost time on the interstate. And I did," she announced, "by speeding most of the way."

"Why did you fly out of New Orleans?" he asked. "I was expecting you to come out of Mississippi."

"Better connections," she answered, and hugged his arm. "Why do you think I'm so interested in a pilot?"

He laughed and said, "Now the truth comes out. It was the airplane that won your heart more than me. That's why you were so mad when you ended up in the middle of Virginia. You were missing the plane, not me." Though he laughed, Marcus felt there was some truth to his teasing.

"That's about as far off course as you were in your opinion of me the day we met."

"Sure?" He frowned at her. When she had disappeared with Paul in Washington, he had been angry, afraid that he had let his emotions get out of control with a woman who was a user. Paul's explanation for their trip into Virginia had practically confirmed that. But whenever he remembered the silky feel of her body trembling against his, he couldn't believe she could be that cold and calculating. That might be the kind of woman Paul was used to dealing with, but Tara had been different. But the more he thought of her, particularly in these last weeks, the more of a dream she had become to him. How could he have been so lucky as to attract a woman like Tara? She fit the life-style Paul was accustomed to living. It was only by association through his former employer that Marcus chanced to be in that world to meet her. And even if she wanted to stay with him, how could he keep her?

"Just give me half a chance and I'll prove my intentions to you," she said seductively.

His heart wanted to believe what he heard, but his logic told him not to be so sure. How would he feel introducing her to his friends as "the doctor"? As much as he wanted to fool himself otherwise, he just didn't think he stood a chance against the men of her experience.

She continued to explain her day. "I raced to New Orleans and found the parking area near the airport disrupted for some kind of repairs. Ten minutes before my flight was called, I was riding the shuttle from the lot to the airport. Then I had to run through the concourse just as they were making the final call for my flight."

"It sounds as if you've already had your exercise for the day," he said.

"Definitely."

"I guess that changes my plans for tonight," he said, and glanced at her half seriously. Thoughts of making love to her had filled his head for weeks. Their coming together in lovemaking, their finding that they could be so compatible, so expressive with one another, had been a wild lark. But she was probably that way with a lot of men, he had told himself.

She caught the devilment in his eyes struggling with the doubts. A spear of desire flashed through her. He was as uncertain as she was about what they would rediscover with each other. It was as if they were meeting for the first time and had never made love. "My stamina is remarkable," she responded with a shaky laugh. No expectations, she reminded herself. But it did nothing to quell the increasing desire she felt surging through her just from his look.

They stopped beside a gray van that had once been silver in its better days. Tara put her hands on his shoulders and begged him for a kiss. He dropped her bag and folded her in his arms as she closed her eyes, reliving every kiss he had given her and the nights they had spent together. This was where she belonged and where she wanted to stay. Somehow she would make him see that. She concentrated on Marcus and the delight she felt in his arms. He filled her mind and her soul and her heart. "I'm so glad I'm here," she whispered.

His arms tightened as if to agree, but he didn't say a word. When he finally released her, he was smiling, and she could read his thoughts in his eyes. He was happy to have her with him.

He unlocked the door and helped her into the passenger seat, then tossed her luggage in the back of the van. Once behind the wheel, it took several attempts before the engine flared to life. He apologized for the rumbling noise of the muffler. "It needs to go into the shop, but I've been more concerned with job hunting than anything else lately. And I didn't want to spend the money."

Tara took that as an opportunity to delve deeper into the subject. "How's that going? Any leads?"

He shook his head. She saw his jaw tighten, the muscle pulsing near his temple. Later, she promised herself, she'd make him talk about it, when the atmosphere was right. She could feel his tension and guessed that he hadn't vented his feelings. She knew the damage bottled emotions could cause.

Tara admired his profile and the warmth of his hand as it rested on her thigh. Her feelings for him hadn't changed, and that excited her. It was still Marcus who interested her, not the background of island beaches, English pubs or European hotels. The sight of his ancient van in normal surroundings somehow seemed more comforting than the starched comfort of elegant hotel rooms or Paul's limousine service.

"I thought we'd go out to dinner before we went back to my place," Marcus said casually. He was uneasy about being alone with her and wanted to delay the moment of showing her his apartment. It wasn't the Dorchester or the Hotel Cravat. There wasn't even a swimming pool or a palm tree to conjure up images of Bermuda. She would probably be disappointed. "You have a couple of surprises in store."

"I love surprises," she assured him, wishing whatever the surprise was, it would have taken place at his home where they could be alone together. He probably wanted to show her Houston, she thought. She was concerned about money being spent on her when he needed to conserve his resources. "But it's enough just to be with you. I'm easily satisfied."

He glanced curiously at her. His ex-wife had said that before she drove out of the marriage with a brand-new car and all of the furniture they had purchased together. Could Tara be different? She was more mature, better educated, but still a woman—as Paul had pointed out. And all the women whom he had ever cared about had been unpredictable.

He shook his head free of Paul. He had put up with his power tactics long enough. When he walked out on his job, he should have left all of Paul's notions behind, too. But there had been an element of truth in things Paul had said not only about Tara but about Marcus's inadequate education and how it would affect him in finding another job. Every place he had tried the past few weeks had turned him down. They had taken one look at his record with the Redding firm, noticed the fine print spelling out his sparse education and said, in effect, "Wise up before you try us again." He wasn't going to let anyone or anything hold him back and had decided to do something about his inadequacies. But he had told himself he was going to forget that for this weekend. Tara had been in town less than an hour, and he couldn't put his problems aside for one evening.

He pulled into the parking lot of a small French restaurant and helped her with the door. The minute she put her hand in his, he couldn't take his eyes off her. She slipped out of the van into his arms. They couldn't keep their hands off each other. It was no

different from the first time he had kissed her, helping her down off that rock in Norway. He sighed
against her. At least that hadn't changed between
them. Smiling as he managed to force his insecurities
aside and put some space between them, he took her
hand and led her inside.

"George!" Tara said when they reached the table
Marcus had reserved for them. She hugged the roly-
poly accountant and smiled at Marcus. "So this is my
surprise. It's wonderful to see you again."

"When Marcus told me you were coming to town,"
he said, setting aside the snack he had ordered while
waiting for them to arrive, "we agreed we should
make this a reunion. Just like old times."

She took the chair Marcus held for her. "I feel
doubly lucky to have both of you here." Not one of
them missed Paul. It *was* good to see George again,
Tara thought, but she had envisioned spending a romantic evening for two with Marcus. Later, she told
herself as they laughed and joked about Tara's last two
days of real hitchhiking and she told George the story
of her opponent, Dick. Over dinner she heard
George's version of their departure from Washington, minus Paul. She started getting angry again at the
things Paul had made up about her. Remembering her
professionalism, she held her anger in check and listened to George talk about the new firm he was with.
He was glad to get back to a job where he could concentrate on accounting and not have the extra duties
Paul tacked on to everyone's job. Tara watched Marcus's reaction carefully to determine how George's
job, and Marcus's lack of one, affected him. But
Marcus held his emotions tightly in control, although
she did notice the pulse at his temple as his jaw tensed.

She couldn't detect any signs of envy or anger directed toward George and guessed that Marcus, too, was irritated about Paul.

It was late by the time they left the restaurant. George gave her another heavy squeeze and kissed her on the cheek. Tara was tired and wondered if Marcus had planned things to be that way in an attempt to avoid intimacy with her. *You're playing psychologist,* she warned herself. *Just be a woman with Marcus. Leave the professional at home.*

Anticipation made her eager by the time they drove up to his small apartment complex. Marcus turned off the key and faced her. "It's not much, but it's where I live," he apologized. In a lighthearted manner, he said, "I figured if the van didn't impress you, this place would."

Tara laughed. The noise of the muffler on the drive to the apartment had totally destroyed the sleepiness the late meal had created. "It doesn't matter," she said, touching his arm. "You couldn't fail to impress me if you tried. I came here to see you."

Marcus wanted to trust in the sincerity he saw in her eyes, but there were still so many things she didn't know about him. His life was so unsettled. Meeting her seemed to point out just how unstable it was.

He unlocked the apartment door and held it open, waiting to see what her reaction would be. She walked into the two-room efficiency and turned, waiting for him. Marcus flipped the light switch, which activated the lamps near the bed and director's chair. They bathed the room in a reddish glow that made it look more exotic than it did during the full light of day. What little furniture he had were quality pieces, but most of his money had gone into a savings account for the business he wanted to start one day. Tara hardly paid attention to the appointments; she kept her eyes on Marcus as he set her bag on the bed and offered her a drink from the selection of bottles he kept near the stereo system.

She smiled and shook her head, then held out her hand to him. "I'm not thirsty or hungry," she said. "I don't want or need anything, Marcus, except you."

He took her hand, deciding not to question her statement, refusing to ask himself how he had expected her to react. She was here, with him, after weeks of separation. How many times had he dreamed of this moment? It wasn't a dream any longer. It was real. "I don't deserve you," he said as he took her into his arms and then led her to his bed.

TARA AWOKE the next morning to a tangle of sheets, feeling Marcus cuddling her in his arms. She stroked his smooth chest and tugged teasingly at the sparse hairs. He sighed in his sleep and tightened his hold on her. She smiled and explored the two rooms of his apartment as well as she could see them from the position she lay in, her cheek pressed against his chest.

The part of the apartment that the bed occupied was small, but it served as the living, dining and sleeping area. The bed took up most of the space and was close to the wall at her back. That wall was lined with books and record albums. His passion for reading matched her own love of books, but she had already guessed that from his knowledge of English history. The opposite side of the room, which she could see, had a closet that one walked through to reach the bath. The kitchen was in an alcove adjacent to the front door.

A chair and a love seat were squeezed into the remaining area of the room. An odd assortment of tables served whatever need was called for—from dining surface to clutter catchall. Tara smiled. The cramped quarters were designed to suit his creature comforts with little space for anything frivolous or for show. She stared at the couch. The lopsided cushions wouldn't make for comfortable necking. She felt somewhat reassured that Marcus probably hadn't spent much time seducing women here. But before the weekend was over, she would make a point of testing out the springs of the couch in a calculated effort to seduce *him*. She didn't think he'd put up much of a fight after the way they had melted in each other's arms before sleep the previous night. Imagining how she would make best use of the couch, she noticed that the cushions were lopsided, because something was stuffed underneath one of them.

She lifted her head to get a better look. The spine of a book was showing. She could barely make out the title. Something on American history.

Marcus felt her stirring and roused himself out of his pleasant dozing. He'd been aware of Tara in his arms all through the night. Once he had awakened and stared at her peaceful face for at least an hour before falling asleep again. He hadn't wanted to move, to wake up to the day ahead. He just wanted to keep feeling her next to him, aware that she was half dream, half reality. When he opened his eyes, she was smiling at him.

"Good morning," she said, forgetting the book in the pleasure emanating from his look.

He put his hand to her cheek. This was real; he hadn't dreamed that she was in his bed as he had so often since the last night they'd spent together in Luxembourg. He cupped the back of her neck and brought her cheek to his, nuzzling against her.

His tenderness filled her heart. She felt a warm bath of arousal stealing over her and began stroking the length of his side. Down the solid bones of his ribs, the softer flesh of his side, to the hard jut of his hips. He turned so that her gentling hand encountered the evidence of his arousal. She laughed softly against his ear, because they were coming to know each other so well, yet there was still the fresh excitement of discovery each time they made love.

It would be so easy, she thought, to whisper, "I love you." But she held back. She didn't want to say it and expect to hear it back. Words were too easy. She wanted him to know without her saying the words, just as she wanted to blossom with the knowledge of his love for her. The unspoken words urged her into a deeper expression of their meaning. She wanted him to feel her love swelling within her heart. She snuggled closer and began tantalizing him in ways she was coming to learn that he loved.

He mumbled little sounds of pleasure that encouraged her to tease and caress him more ardently. As his hands played gently over her back, she seduced him with her lips, pressing kisses against his neck, to his throat and down, ever downward to his delight.

"You're doing that on purpose," he murmured, kissing the tender area inside her elbow and massaging that secret area above her shoulder blade that he had discovered pleased her.

"You'd better believe it," she said, smiling during her loving ministrations as he grew increasingly aroused. She concentrated on pleasing him, knowing that he would give her equal attention eventually or that their lovemaking would turn into a mutually satisfying passion. It never followed a pattern, although they were discovering more about each other's needs and desires each time they came together.

Before the pleasure was too great, Marcus interrupted her, lifting her slight body onto his chest, spreading her thighs with his ankle locking around hers. She opened to him, accepting him with a gasp of pure happiness, rocking with the rhythm of his lead.

She closed her eyes, feeling him, all of him, deep within her. The passion that their love had created swelled. Marcus watched her face, knowing that she was reaching the brink to which she had brought him. He kept stroking her, urging the rhythms faster. Passion was growing and pushing at her, as if someone were inflating balloons, party balloons in a multitude of colors, each one increasing in dimension, expanding the depths of her love for Marcus until she thought she would burst. He felt her moment of impossible tension as she caught her breath, as if she had stopped on the path he was leading her. And then she was with him as they raced headlong into each other with a splash of light and laughter and love.

They lay with their bodies entwined, savoring the afterglow. And Tara thought that surely no two people were better suited to each other. Marcus tugged tenderly at her curls, wanting her but thinking of the impossibility of their situation. If only the rest of their lives could be as well matched as their lovemaking, he thought, he might stand a chance with her. But there were too many gaps. He was smart enough to know that even the best of lovers couldn't live on love alone.

Chapter Eleven

Dear Tara,
    I love waking up with you in my bed. How did
I ever make it through the night without you?

                                        Marcus

While Marcus was in the shower, Tara made the
bed, smiling at the note he had left on the pillow. She
picked up her clothes, which had gotten scattered the
night before, and repacked everything in her suitcase.
Stuffing it out of the way, she tried to keep order in the
small apartment. When she finished, she sat on the
edge of the bed, waiting for Marcus, wondering what
they would do that day. And she noticed the book under the cushion of the couch again.

She tried to imagine what it was doing there. Maybe
there was a dangerous spring that sprouted through
the cushions unless a barrier, like the book, was placed
on top of it. Maybe there were no springs in the couch
and it took a hard object, like the book, to give the
couch support. She had once used a book to support
her bed where one wheel had broken on the frame. Or
maybe—

Tara glanced over her shoulder. She could still hear
the sound of running water in the bathroom. Cross-

ing the narrow space, she tugged the book from its hiding place. It was on American history. She flipped through the pages, staring at it from front to back cover. There were questions at the end of each chapter and points for discussion. It wasn't a library book, because it didn't have a sleeve for a dated card. There was a label on the inside cover indicating that it was on loan from a community college.

Tara lifted the cushion to shove the book out of sight and noticed another book. Curious, she pulled it out. High school English. Another label from the community college, and Marcus's name was the last one on the list of borrowers.

She lifted the cushions all the way, both cushions, and found an algebra text and a science book. More curious than ever, she examined the labels more closely, searching for a date. Could Marcus be going back to school? Why hadn't he told her?

"Are you as hungry as I am?" Marcus called. From the sound of his voice she could tell he had opened the bathroom door. She could even hear the sound of the towel as he dried off.

Frantically, she clutched the incriminating books to her breast. "Uh, yes!" she called. Should she confront him with the books? Could she pretend she hadn't found them without learning why he had hidden them? No, that wouldn't work. He would have left them sitting on the coffee table or on the bookshelves if he hadn't minded her, or anyone else, seeing them. Maybe he always kept them in the couch.

"I thought I'd fix hazelnut muffins and *huevos rancheros* for breakfast." From the strength of his voice, he was in the closest area now. The squeaks from the hangers against the rod told her he was shuffling through his clothes, looking for something to wear.

In her haste to dispose of the evidence, Tara nearly tripped over the coffee table. She dumped the books back into the couch and smoothed the cushions over it. "Sounds great," she called, standing back to look at her efforts. That wouldn't work. The cushions were too even, neater than she had found them. She rearranged them, creating a definite lump in one side. She stood back and smiled. Before the day was over, she would entice him onto the couch and make sure she sat on the lumpy end so that she could complain and "accidentally" uncover the books. She was smiling when he emerged from the closet and bath area a second later, still wearing a towel.

"Did you hear me?" he asked.

"I think so," she said, turning, knowing she was blushing. Maybe he would think it was because he looked so sexy in a towel. "We're hungry, right? I got that part."

He laughed uneasily, looking from her to the couch. "What were you doing?"

"Just admiring the couch," she said, distracting him by removing the towel.

"What's so special about it?" He didn't object to her hands spreading over his chest and across his flat stomach.

"It's an unusual color," she said, laying her lips against his chest, kissing and caressing with her tongue. "Mustard orange."

His hands slid down her back to pull her hips up hard against his. "We'll never eat breakfast if you keep that up." But he made no move to stop her.

"Breakfast? Oh, I was supposed to be hungry, wasn't I?" she said, smiling up at him, her cheeks dimpling. "I forgot."

He liked the playful look in her eyes. One minute she was all seriousness, the next as spritely as a child. It was part of what he loved about her. Without that daring spirit he often saw lurking in her eyes, he might never have met her. He kissed her and moved her gently away from him, retreating to the closet for his clothes.

"It's a good thing one of us knows how to cook," Tara said later as she watched him litter the countertop with bowls, utensils and ingredients for the breakfast feast.

He arched an eyebrow in her direction, and the corner of his mouth went up in a half smile.

Grinning, she bent to put her elbows on the countertop, watching him work. He beat the eggs with a wire whisk and eyed her warily. To distract both of them from her questions about the couch and the books hidden there, Tara talked about her classes. Since the hitchhiking contest, she had felt more like a part of the group, but as before, studying gave her little time to socialize with the others. She hoped mentioning studying would make him talk about the books in the couch. It didn't. "Once I start the work involved in applying for my internship," she said, "I'm going to be busier than ever."

"What does that involve?" he asked, adding butter to a heated frying pan.

"First of all, I'll need to narrow down the area of the country I'd like to work in."

"Not in Mississippi?"

"It is a possibility," she said, and hesitated before voicing her latest thoughts on the topic. "But I had been thinking more of San Francisco. The climate's temperate, and the opportunities in my field are more numerous. And then there's Florida. You remember how much I enjoyed the beach in Bermuda." Those choices had been made before she had met Marcus. "I'm also considering Texas." She didn't add that the Lone Star State had entered her circle of interest after meeting Marcus. She paused, watching closely for his reaction. "Like San Antonio, which I've heard is beautiful, or Austin or Houston."

He took his eyes off of the egg mixture long enough to smile at her. "What happens after you've chosen a site?"

She took a deep breath. He hadn't seemed displeased to know that she could become his neighbor by this time next year. "Well, I have to apply, send letters of recommendation, examples of my work, the usual, just like a job résumé. Then I interview with the places that are interested in me."

His jaw tightened at the mention of job interviews. But of course it would be easier for her with a degree behind her name. "When do you have to make your applications?" he asked.

"Between now and the end of the year," she said, adding, "If I interview in Texas, at least I'd have a legitimate excuse for seeing you again."

"A legitimate excuse for an illegitimate rendezvous," he said, chuckling. He stopped beating the eggs long enough to bend over and kiss her. He smiled at her reaction. "What happens after that?"

"Final decisions are made on the thirteenth of February. All around the country, no one leaves their phone that day."

"What happens if more than one place wants you?" Right now he'd be happy if one firm wanted his services.

"Then it's up to me to say yes to the one I want the most. By that point I should have my mind made up as to my first and second choices. You can't keep anyone on hold about your decision much longer than a day."

Choices. That's what education gave you. Without it he had to take whatever came along, *if* something opened up. "If I understand this correctly," he said, proving that he had been closely following Tara's explanations, "you could move anywhere in the country?"

"Yes," she said. "I'm only living in Mississippi because of the university. By this time next year I'll be settled in a new place."

Time had never been a luxury for him. Marcus had always been forced to earn a living, for his family, his wife, himself. There had never been time for an education. And now, at thirty-seven years old, it had caught up with him. His ex-wife had been right when she had said he would never amount to anything. "For how long?" He concentrated on what she was saying.

"Internships generally last a year. But if I enjoy the area well enough, I could stay longer. Very often you're offered a job to continue where you are. Either way, my degree will give me the opportunity to move anywhere I'd like to."

Her education meant choices and freedom. She could go anywhere she wanted to. He was forced to go where the job took him, if he could find a job. "Where would you like to live?"

Her eyes said, *Anywhere you are,* but she responded, "I'm not sure." She remembered when she had asked him the same thing. "What I'd like to do is become a consultant for top management—setting up personnel systems or counseling. The reason I decided to go back to school was to get out of the nine-to-five office routine. I'd like to have more flexibility with my schedule." *Now,* she thought, *if he knew that I knew about the books he doesn't want me to know about, I could ask him about them.* She resisted the urge to look over her shoulder at the couch. Wrong timing. She'd have to wait for another opportunity to turn the subject of school over to him. It would be so easy to ask, "Have you ever tried going back to school, Marcus?"

He couldn't stop thinking of their differences due to education. "What are you staring at?" he asked.

"What? Oh. Do you put cinnamon in that?"

"In the eggs?" He gave her a confused glance.

"No. In the, uh, muffins?"

He shook his head. "I guess you weren't kidding when you said it was a good thing one of us could cook. What do you eat when you're at home?"

"I've always managed to find a roommate who cooks." She grinned, blowing at her bangs because she had let the question of the books eat at her. She had to put them out of her mind for now or she would spoil this lovely moment with him.

"What about before you went back to school? Did you live in Massachusetts with a man who cooked?"

Bad subject, she thought. What had gone before for both of them was ancient history. Oh, blast, she thought, would she ever get that *history* book out of her mind? What mattered was building something with Marcus now, moving forward from this point in time. Something told her those books were going to be a stumbling block. She was anxious to talk about that, but she had to introduce the topic gently. "I was married," she answered, "like you were, remember? It wasn't one of my favorite times."

He nodded, wisely deciding not to pursue the subject. They had talked a little about their ex-mates while in Europe. Marriage had happened a long time ago for both of them. But both of them were still dealing with the aftereffects of the union. The eggs went into the pan as the oven timer rang.

"I'll get the muffins," Tara offered while he tended to the eggs. She shook them out of the tins onto a plate, then stood behind Marcus, locking her arms around him, resting her head against his back as he cooked. He grasped her forearm to reinforce her hug while his other hand lifted the edges of the eggs with a spatula. *This is love,* she thought, feeling the reassurance of his grasp. It comes in little moments, not from monumental declarations that are broadcast for the hearing. Marcus hadn't spoken a word of love to her, nor she to him. They hadn't exchanged promises or hopes, yet love wrapped them in warmth together.

During breakfast, Marcus talked objectively about the places he had been seeking a job. He spoke as impersonally as if he were reading listings from the phone directory. Tara sensed the frustration building from the tone of his voice.

"Has it occurred to you that Paul might have spread the word ahead of you, out of spite, just to make certain you never get a job in your field in this town?"

"That's crossed my mind more than once."

"After all, you got the job with Paul with less experience than you have today."

"Times were different then," he said. His fingers tapped the table nervously. As a counselor, she knew they were getting close to the source of his irritation. She didn't interrupt so that he would continue talking. "There's more emphasis on degrees these days. You're a perfect example. You're going to be a doctor." He stared at her as if it were a crime; then his eyes shifted away from her. He had told himself he wouldn't let his lack of education come between them. After a minute he got up and started carrying their plates into the kitchen.

Tara watched him clattering the dishes in the sink and didn't make a move to help. The anger she had seen in his eyes was simmering closer to the surface. If she could get him to let it out, she'd understand better why it was directed toward her. As loving as Marcus had been in bed, there were walls between them that hadn't existed that summer. She had suspected it when he hadn't immediately taken her home from the airport, felt it even stronger with George's presence at dinner and sensed Marcus had danced around intimacy that morning with the elaborate preparations for a breakfast that had taken less than fifteen minutes to eat. As a counselor, Tara had learned to let a patient talk it out of themselves instead of accusing or prodding toward anger. But as a woman in love with Marcus, it was difficult to keep her feelings out of it. She wanted to bounce on the couch, unearth the books and wave them in his face. Instead, she said calmly, "Have you thought of looking for a job in Dallas or Amarillo or—"

"Paul Redding is not going to run me out of town," he said, turning on her. "He doesn't own me, and he doesn't own this town." Tara was thinking of George and how easily he had found another job because of his skills and his degrees. As if reading her mind, Marcus continued, "George had the education, the aptitude and the Redding name to help him get past any conniving of Paul's making. But I still say experience counts for something—for a lot. And I intend to prove it."

"To whom?" Tara asked. "To Paul, who couldn't give a damn? Or to yourself? What's the point, Marcus?"

"Anything I do won't mean a hill of beans if I act on someone else's puppet strings. I can't do a thing for you or for Paul or for anyone if it doesn't mean something to me first."

"Marcus, I've never asked you to prove anything to me."

"You don't have to ask. Who you are as a person asks enough in itself."

"What do you mean by that?"

"Your degrees. Your college education. Your status. How do you think I can ever measure up to that? Will I have to call you 'Doctor' whenever I introduce you to my friends? Would you even lower yourself to want to meet my friends? We come from two different worlds, Tara. Yours is up there somewhere on a cloud, out of reach for me."

"It seems to me as if you've flown some pretty high clouds yourself, Marcus," she said, all of her attempts at professionalism shattered. She loved him and had no defenses against him. All she knew was somehow she had to make him understand his importance in her life. The way he was talking made her feel as if he were looking for a way to end the relationship before it had properly begun.

"If you're talking about the airplane, that's poetic. Thanks."

"Marcus," she began, "your talent lies in flying. If I spent the rest of my life studying books, I couldn't begin to know all that you do in that area. 'Doctor' is simply a label. It appears incidentally in my field. And anyway, after all of the work I'm going through to earn my title, everyone's going to call me Tara, as they've always done."

"It's not the same thing."

"No," she agreed, "it's not. Your status lies in the number of hours you've accumulated from flying and from the different types of planes you can fly. It comes from all of the knowledge you've acquired about flight and aerodynamics. And how many pilots are qualified to fly internationally? That's definitely way over my head. That doesn't make what you do any less important, especially to me. But if you're going to let that difference come between us, then maybe you're not the man I thought you were." His glare prompted her to add, "Are you using our educational backgrounds as an excuse to avoid a relationship? It didn't seem to matter this summer when we were together."

He wanted to deny the truth of what she said. Education had been at the root of his marriage breaking up. "It was there," he stated. "Neither one of us had any idea we'd see each other again. For two weeks we weren't in my world or yours. We were in this never-never land of Europe and glamorous travel. As long as I held my fork and spoon correctly, no one was going to guess at my inadequacies. But things are different now. Every bit of my background comes to light and is examined. And I keep falling short.''

Marcus had more courage and integrity than he gave himself credit for. She had to make him see that.

He faced her. "Look at this," he said, his arm sweeping the apartment. "I'm thirty-seven years old, and I'm still struggling to find my place in the structure of business. I don't even have a decent place to live because I've tried to save everything extra to buy my own plane one day. But now that I'm out of work, I have to dig into those savings.''

"There's nothing wrong with that," she said. "You have goals. You know what you want. Most people don't even see that they have a future ahead of them.''

"But I'm never going to make it to the top of the corporate structure the way Paul Redding has done.''

"So what? You'd be miserable if you did. That's not what you want for yourself, so you shouldn't feel badly that you won't reach that point.''

"Most of the men you date are probably executives who can just sit back and pick up a check from their profits each month.''

"Is that what you think?''

"It's true, isn't it?''

She couldn't deny it. Paul Redding did fall into the class of men she was accustomed to going out with. But Marcus was different. He gave her intangible gifts that were far more valuable than any material trinkets Paul could ever buy for her, like tenderness and sensitivity, and he shared his feelings with her. "Don't you see?'' she said. "What you're working toward makes more sense than anything Paul could do. You're climbing a different structure. Your success is going to be much more valuable than Paul's. He's the type of man who has always had everything handed to him on a silver platter. When you never had to work for it, it makes that platter about as worthless as tinfoil."

He paced into the living area, with Tara dogging his steps. "College professors earn a lot less money than I'll be making once I'm in private practice," she said. "Does the money make me smarter? They have degrees, too, you know. Does it make the corporate executive, like Paul, more intelligent than a high school teacher?"

"It's apples and oranges," he grumbled.

"Exactly," she said. "School isn't the best answer for some people, Marcus. All of learning doesn't come from books." She smiled as she sensed understanding growing between them. "And if it's any consolation, your apartment fits right in with my life-style."

He blinked. "How?"

"My roommate, Julie, is the one who has all of the furniture. I brought a few pieces with me when I moved to Mississippi. If I had more furniture, I wouldn't be half as willing to accept the risks it takes to climb the ladder of recognition in my field. I haven't been ready to reestablish roots, either." She smiled. "You're doing the same thing I am, just in a different manner."

"And how am I doing that?" he asked. "I don't even have a job right now. I don't see how you can stand there and make comparisons between us."

"I was talking about going back to school."

He stared at her. "What do you know about that?" He walked back into the kitchen as if he wanted to escape her answer.

"Enough to know it takes a lot of courage to go back to school at any point in your life, but particularly when you're older. It takes real dedication and a lot of hard work to develop study habits. You didn't decide to do it because anyone forced you. You're not expecting people to be impressed if you can wave that diploma in their faces or not."

"How do you know what I feel about that?" he asked, realizing that it *had* been his decision to go back to school. He hadn't told her because he wanted her to be proud of him when he finished. If he had wanted her approval, he would have asked her advice. As comprehension dawned, he accused, "You weren't just admiring the color of that couch this morning."

She lifted her shoulders nonchalantly and admitted, "Actually I was trying to devise ways to seduce you on the couch so that I could complain about the lumpy books beneath my back."

His eyes darted from her to the couch, to the bed and back again, resting on her. Then he laughed.

"You should have given me a chance to try out my plan," she teased, her eyes dancing mischievously. "The books are nothing to be ashamed of, Marcus. I don't know why you'd want to hide them."

"Because I thought you'd laugh if I told you," he said. "I mean, what's a high school diploma compared to what you're working toward at that university?"

"Probably a lot more effort for you than my studies are. And anyway, if you were an exact mirror of myself, there wouldn't be anything exciting to discover between us."

"I'll admit I never seriously thought about going back to school until I met you this summer. There just never seemed to be the time. But *I* made the decision. You're right about that."

"You probably thought about it a lot more than you realize," she said. "I'm just happy if I was a catalyst for you in making that decision."

His eyes tugged at her soul. "Do you know how special you are to me?"

She went to him then and stepped into his open arms. Words could not express her need for him or how, by being with her, he had given her life new meaning. They held each other, afraid to break the spell that bound them in a web of caring. She wanted to tell him then that she loved him, but like the time he had avoided kissing her because he wanted the setting and the kiss to be memorable, she waited. She didn't want him to remember that they were standing in front of a sink filled with dirty dishes after having their first argument.

"You were going to seduce me on the couch, huh?" he asked.

She rested her chin on his chest and smiled up at him. "I just love the brute strength of your brain." He chuckled, and she asked, "Tell me about your school."

He took her hand then and led her to the couch but removed the books from beneath the cushions before they sat. "I like math and working with figures. It's like a universal language. All of the calculations that go with flying have been a breeze for me. So that's my easier subject. I guess that's one of the reasons I'd like to see the figures stacking up in my own business one day. Science is close to a lot I've had to learn to earn my pilot's license, so that's a breeze. And I like history. But the English gives me fits. All those papers. And it's so degrading to be sent home with red check marks when you're as old as I am but you didn't know to put a comma in the right place."

"At least you don't get kept after school," she said with a laugh, and put her arms around his neck. "Please don't give me a superiority complex. I don't deserve one. Besides, I came all of this distance just to feel your arms around me."

He pulled her closer then, all of the argument going out of him. "I still have a lot of things to straighten out in my life, like a job to begin with. But maybe you're right. The smartest thing I can do this weekend is to get down to some heavy sensualization."

"Sensualization?" she said, laughing as he nuzzled her ear. "At the risk of sounding supercilious, I don't think there's such a word."

"You can be super anything you want," he promised, and smiled. "But if you don't know the meaning of the word, maybe I'd better show you."

Chapter Twelve

Tara thought the work had piled up in her absence, although she hadn't missed a day of classes with her visit to Texas. There were so many books to read, papers to write, interviews to do and tests to study for. Two days after her return she felt as if she had been buried in books for two weeks without a break. By the end of the week, her time with Marcus seemed more distant, more of a dream. The only reality were the words in front of her, the classes of instruction and the number of résumés she had to get in the mail.

She had talked more in depth with Marcus that weekend about doing her internship in Texas. If she hadn't met Marcus, San Francisco would still have been her first choice. The letters of application to Texas remained on her desk for several days while she vacillated in her decision. The positions looked challenging, and she would know more about them if called in for an interview, but what bothered her was that she was putting her feelings for Marcus before the practicality of her career. If she sent the letters, received an offer and moved to Texas, it would be due to Marcus's presence there. It made her feel as if she were less the master of her own career. How many times had she counseled women not to make a move solely because of a man? When the relationship fell apart, the woman was left in a strange environment with her only friend—the ex-lover—no longer part of her life.

But this was different, Tara reasoned. Her internship would only last a year. If she didn't like the work or things fell through with Marcus, she could move on, putting that segment of her life behind her. Besides, all of the positions were top-notch in her field; they just weren't in San Francisco. But if Marcus were around, she could get run over by a cable car and not notice the surroundings. Finally, she picked up the letters intended for Texas and mailed them. She would let the fates decide. Texas might not be interested in *her*. And she was still a long way from making that final decision of accepting the best job after the best offer.

Class work mounted. Even the weekly chats with Marcus by phone did little to help. He still hadn't found a job, but his own schoolwork was continuing. Tara was glad that he had that to keep him busy. He was pouring all of his attention into his books to help speed up the process. "We're like two college kids who have both gone away from home to school," Tara said with a laugh one night.

"Except that home is where you are whenever we're together," Marcus corrected. "And I'm missing you."

"That's nice to hear," Tara said, "but I don't want you spending the money coming over here when your finances are still unsettled. And I'm so overwhelmed with work that I'd probably be reading over your shoulder the whole time you were here."

He chuckled. "Maybe so, but I bet it would be a *bare* shoulder. You know you can feel free to read lying on top of me anytime you get the urge."

"I'm feeling a lot of urges lately, and they all have your name on them."

With her studies, her indecision over internship and her concern about Marcus's job situation, Tara slipped into a schedule that allowed little time for socializing. The triumphs from the hitchhiking adventure were gradually fading. She realized she was deliberately isolating herself from the other students again, but this time it was because of her preoccupation with other matters. She had barely seen Julie, who spent most nights studying with her boyfriend. She and Julie left notes for each other in the kitchen and passed each other in the halls of the Ed-Psych building. Rarely did they even have time for a cup of morning coffee together.

This has got to change, Tara decided one day after she had stayed up until three A.M. to meet a deadline on a paper. Aside from studying, she was spending more time at home just in case Marcus called more than his customary one or two times a week. When she had a problem, she would ordinarily have discussed it with Julie; now she phoned Marcus. He never gave her advice; he just listened, which was all that she would have wanted Julie to do, anyway. He was an absent entity in her life around which everything revolved. She had even begun to hope that San Francisco wouldn't ask her to interview so that she wouldn't be torn making decisions when Texas called, as she was sure would happen.

Half of her resented the importance Marcus had taken in her life. The other half recognized that the relationship that could evolve with Marcus was something she had longed for all of her life. The timing between them just seemed inconvenient. With her degree a year away, her career was still unsettled. Marcus was out of a job. They weren't even close enough to see each other on weekends. Yet when they had been together, he had satisfied her in a way that she had never dreamed any man could.

There was no doubt in her mind that she loved him. But she couldn't understand why she hadn't been able to tell him that. Was she being childish in wanting to hear him say the words first? Was she afraid of the commitment the words implied? Or was the timing just plain wrong? She didn't want to tell him something so important over the phone. She wanted to watch his eyes when she said, "I love you."

Practically, she did her best to divorce her mind from him in order to stay focused on her studies. And she talked with Julie about having a party on Friday evening to break the monotony of study for the grad students. Tara was determined not to lose touch with her friends because of her absorption with Marcus. "Sounds great," Julie agreed. "We haven't had one party all semester. Let's get a cake—That reminds me. It's Della's birthday Monday. We can make it a semi-surprise prebirthday party for her."

"And Sally and Alec just got engaged."

"An engagement party, too," Julie said, her eyes shining with excitement. "Let's see. What other things can we think of to celebrate?"

"Friday."

Julie laughed. "You're right. That's celebration enough. What a week this has been." She picked up a pad and began making notes of things they would need for the party. She looked up from her scribblings. "Why don't we invite some of the new kids that came into the department this year?"

"Sure. The more the merrier. It might break the ice between some of the cliques the old-timers around here have set up. I'll check with the rental center in town. I bet we can get some cheap wineglasses. I hate drinking out of plastic cups."

"Great idea." Julie wrote it down. "I'll pass the word that it's a pot-luck, bring-your-own supper. There's always more food than we need that way."

Tara became more excited as the plans for the party developed. It was just the diversion she needed to re-establish friendships and forget the books for a few hours. That it was practically a last-minute suggestion gave her little time to back out or concern herself with the thought of the chores that would come afterward during the cleanup. It gave her a lift when most of the other students said they would be there.

The sidewalk was lined with candles set in sand and paper bags, the way the historic homes were decorated in town during Christmas. The table was set to display a spread of food. Tara had splurged on champagne in honor of the engaged couple. Julie had ordered the birthday cake, which would be unveiled to reveal a top-heavy naked lady, since Della was always complaining about being so flat chested. Julie and Tara had rearranged the furniture the night before to give the living area plenty of room for milling and mingling guests. The tape deck was cued to play the first of several tapes selected for background music.

There wasn't anything left to do but change clothes and wait for the arrival of the guests, Tara decided. Julie still wasn't home from class and would probably be late for the party because of a previous commitment. Tara had decided to present a sophisticated image at one of the school parties for a change and planned to wear a sleek black cocktail dress to remind everyone she wasn't the stuffy old student who didn't know how to have a good time, not after her hard-earned victory that summer.

She checked Julie's antique clock near the stereo and decided she had enough time for a quick nap before she began dressing. Tara stretched out on the couch with her feet elevated by the side arm and sighed. Preparations for the party, thrown into the middle of an otherwise-busy week, had given her little time to think. Now, with the quiet repose, thoughts rushed forward. Marcus hadn't phoned that week. She had tried to reach him twice but hadn't received a response either time. She wondered if he would phone that evening during the party. Or maybe his phone had been disconnected because he was no longer able to pay his bill. As much as it concerned her, she had to let him work out his career problems on his own. She had offered suggestions and been supportive, but there wasn't much else he would allow her to do, even if she could. She smiled, admiring that about Marcus. He was his own man. He wasn't going to let anyone get the better of him, particularly Paul Redding. But he had certainly given himself tough obstacles to overcome the day he had flown out of Washington without his boss.

The doorbell rang. Tara jumped and looked at the clock. It was too early for the guests to be arriving, and Julie never used that door even when she forgot her key. She glanced down at her lounging jumpsuit and decided that if it was an early party guest, she would at least be halfway in the spirit to greet them.

Marcus stood on the doorstep. For a minute Tara just stared; then, unable to contain her emotions, she hurled herself at him, hugging his neck. As his arms came around her, lifting her feet off the floor, she locked her legs around his waist, giving him the full weight of her body. "What are you doing here?" she asked. "I've been trying to call you all week." She buried her face against his neck, luxuriating in the feel of him.

"I wanted to surprise you," he said, laughing, gently setting her down, loving the warm response she gave him.

"You did."

"I don't know about that," he said, grinning at her and looking around the room. "I think I'm the one who's more surprised. What's going on here?"

"Oh," Tara said, her hand flying to her throat. "We're having a party. I thought you were an early guest. Oh, Marcus, I'm so glad to see you." She took his hand. "Come in."

He picked up his bag and set it inside the door, following her into the living area. "I guess I should have called you," he said, looking around at the room, mixed with modern furniture and antiques. It made his place look like something out of a cardboard cutout. Balloons were strung across the mantel, and streamers hung from the chandelier. "But I didn't think you'd be doing anything but studying and—"

She tugged at his hand for him to sit on the couch beside her. She tucked her leg beneath her and faced him. "Seeing you is the most wonderful surprise I've *ever* had."

"I don't want to interrupt anything, but I couldn't wait any longer to see you."

"It's just a party, Marcus. It'll be even more fun with you here. You're not interrupting anything." She laughed. "But you might be regretting the surprise visit later when Julie and I put you to work to clean up the mess."

He smiled, unable to take his eyes off the objects decorating the room, and felt like celebrating his good news.

"This is perfect," she said, snuggling up to his arms. "You'll be able to meet all of my friends here in Hattiesburg. They've heard about you from the hitchhiking contest." She rolled her eyes. "You'll have to put up with Dick, too. He'll be here. But meeting him will also give you a greater appreciation for why I was so compelled to beat him this summer. How long can you stay?"

"I thought I'd stay the weekend," he said, "but now—"

"Now you'll stay the weekend," she said firmly. To focus his attention on the reason he had come in the first place, she took his face between her hands and interrupted his appraisal of the room. "Hey," she said. "Remember me?"

He closed his eyes and gathered her into his arms, needing only her. Then she was kissing him, nibbling at the cord of his neck, chasing unwanted thoughts aside as a more basic need of a man to be with a woman stole over his body. She felt smaller than he remembered. Each time they were away from each other was longer than the time before, intensifying his longing for her. But it took only moments to remember what excited her and how her excitement fed his own passion for Tara.

He kissed her, tracing her lips with the tip of his tongue. What was he doing right to keep her? "I don't deserve you," he mumbled, wondering if he could stack up to her friends. He wanted to meet them, but not right then. If he had known about the party, he wouldn't have come. But he had wanted to surprise her, so it was his own fault for not knowing ahead of time that he couldn't be alone with her.

"Marcus," she whispered, "you're worthy of merit in your own way. There's no reason you should feel as if you *deserve* me. I love the sentiment, but you're wrong about this pedestal you're putting me on. We deserve each other." She kissed him. "I'm so happy you're here." She sat back. "What made you decide to come? I mean, I thought you weren't going to spend any money unnecessarily unless—" She smiled. "You got a job!"

He grinned. They knew each other too well. It suddenly made him feel as if he *were* home, with her. He nodded, the grin widening. He had known before he got here that she would be as excited by the news as he had been. And he had waited to share the news when he could see her reaction. He hadn't wanted the impersonality of the phone between them for such important information. "I've been flying all week. It's why you haven't been able to reach me when you tried calling."

"What kind of company is it?"

"A small oil-exploration firm. I'll be flying the executives all over the South and Midwest, but my trips last week were to Oklahoma."

"You should have called. I've been so concerned about you."

"I know," he said, taking her hand, feeling her pulse fluttering in her wrist. "But I just didn't want to break the news that way. When I got the job, I felt like celebrating; but you were the one I wanted to celebrate with, so here I am."

"This is wonderful!" she said, hugging his neck again. "What perfect timing! Now we have a *real* reason to have the party tonight. Julie and I kept thinking up reasons for celebration."

"Tara, I don't know—"

"It's already a combination birthday, engagement, thank-God-it's-Friday party. This is even more important."

"Tara, no," he said firmly. "A party's nice, but I don't want to turn it into a Marcus-finally-got-a-job party."

She understood his sensitivity on the subject, particularly since he would be meeting all of her friends for the first time. "They don't have to know," she assured him. "We know what we're celebrating. That's all that matters." The clock chimed the hour, and Tara glanced over her shoulder. She didn't believe the time. "I have to start getting ready, but I want to hear all of the details. Come talk to me while I dress."

"You might not get dressed if I come talk to you," he warned. It only took looking at her to remember all of the things he missed about her.

"Oh," she said, chewing on her lower lip, then grinning wider. "You're probably right about that. Would it be in bad taste for the hostess to be late for her own party?"

"SALLY, I want you to meet Marcus Landry," Tara said later, taking him by the arm and introducing her fellow student.

"We've met," Marcus said, smiling affectionately at Tara, who made him feel important the way she kept introducing him to everyone. "You introduced us when she arrived with Alec. But I'm happy to meet you again." Graciously he shook her hand, exaggerating the contact.

"Don't mind Tara," Sally said, apologizing to Marcus. "She just wants to show you off." She included Tara in her assessment. "I can't say that I blame you, Tara. If Alec hadn't just asked me to marry him, I might be having second thoughts now that I've met Marcus twice."

"Maybe you should introduce me to Alec again," Marcus suggested to Tara, "just to make it official that I've met both of them." He smiled, not knowing what else to say. He had just met a roomful of people—some of them twice—and he had nothing in common with any of them except for the fact that they all knew Tara. Small talk had never been one of his assets. Years of traveling with Paul Redding had taught him a few conversational tricks, but they had little effect with this highbrow group. "By the way," Marcus added, "in case I didn't say it earlier, congratulations on your engagement."

Sally laughed. "You did mention it, but I love hearing it, so thanks."

Marcus was grateful when Tara nudged his arm and took him to another corner of the room to meet someone else. He hoped it was someone new this time. What little he had to say might come out sounding halfway profound. And he was quickly losing track of who was who, not to mention which couples were together. He couldn't count on Tara to help him. As much as she kept homing back to his side, the duties of a hostess kept taking her away from him. Her roommate, Julie, wasn't there yet, so Tara had to do most of the work. He stood in the corner of the room with a drink in his hand that made him look occupied and wished plants could talk.

In the dining area, which adjoined the living room, everyone was calling for Della. "It's time to cut the cake. Dick's already pointed out the parts he wants." Everyone laughed as Marcus followed the others. He stood on the fringe of the group as they sang, "Happy Birthday and Engagement, Della, Sally and Alec."

"That sounds like a *ménage à trois*," Della said, slicing into the anatomy of the cake's decorations and piling mounds of icing on Dick's plate. Tara was in the middle of things, handing out plates. When she looked his way, Marcus lifted his glass to her as if he were perfectly comfortable in this situation; but he was beginning to wish he had never come. He had pictured spending a quiet evening alone with her, maybe even helping her study while he got ready for his first big exam—for high school.

There was a small group of students nearby discussing coping strategies. Marcus tried eavesdropping on the conversation. He could definitely use some help in coping with this party tonight. He couldn't shake from his mind his ex-wife's taunts about how lack of education would always make him stand out like a sore thumb. He smiled and looked interested in what the students were saying, searching for a chance to join in the conversation.

"Now take the person who knows how to use cognitive restructuring," one student began. "For instance, when a romance falls apart, instead of feeling self-pity or being overwhelmed or upset about the situation, they see it as a plus."

"How's that?" Marcus interrupted. He looked at Tara, acting fully at ease with this houseful· of company, and couldn't imagine feeling anything but upset about losing her. But as his feelings of being out of place kept getting stronger, he thought it might help to get some insights on how to cope with a breakup. His ex-wife would certainly be laughing if she could see him here now.

The student explained for Marcus's benefit, "In cognitive restructuring, the person would direct their energy toward a career and look at what they had gained from the love affair even if it didn't work out."

"On the other hand," another female student spoke up, "someone who uses adaptive refocus energy would call up a support system or take a trip to forget."

"Or they could sublimate," someone else answered. Seeing the blank look on Marcus's face, the student explained, "Direct their creativity, take up sailing, you know, get involved in some activity rather than withdrawing in sleep, you *know*?"

Marcus didn't know, and he was feeling worse about his inability to comprehend their psychological terminology. Damn. What was he doing here? He stepped over to the bar dividing the two rooms and selected a bottle of Italian wine to refill his glass. Tasting, he decided he didn't like it. He finished it in two swallows and searched among the bottles for something else. He was quickly forgetting why he had come here in the first place.

While Tara had finished dressing after they had
spent an all-too-short time together in bed, Marcus
had explored the house's two rooms that were hers.
The bedroom was as crammed as his, with a bed,
dressing cabinet and bookshelves. It was the other
room that had fascinated him. She had turned it into
a study complete with two desks, a typewriter, a com-
puter, an easy chair and more shelves. There were
books and papers everywhere, open, as she had left
them on the floor around the typing chair, and stacked
with bookmarks beside the desk. It made his reading,
writing and arithmetic look like the ABCs. He remembered how his ex-wife had laughed at the books
he had bought. *Reading won't make up for schooling,* she had said.

Dick Shaw was creating uneasy laughter near the
buffet table, lapping at the mounds of icing as if they
were the anatomy they represented. Someone nearby
was spouting the merits of intrinsic versus extrinsic
exchange. Marcus felt his head swimming. He looked
at the glass of wine in his hand. He listened long
enough to hear both sides of the argument and still
didn't know what they were talking about.

Tara came up beside Marcus. He smiled at her as if
he were having a good time. She took his arm and put
it around her. He stood rigidly beside her, listening to
the conversations around him. If he reeled out a series of weight and balance calculations for them to
figure out, he could bet they would be as stymied as he
was in their field. He could work figures in his head
almost as well as a calculator. But they probably
wouldn't be the least impressed. Marcus stared at Tara
as if he suddenly noticed he had his arm around a rat-
tlesnake. "I don't belong here," he muttered, just

loud enough for her to hear. Then he stalked back to the liquor counter.

Tara followed him. He had been strangely quiet all evening, reminding her of the first evening they had spoken together. They had been on the yacht in Norfolk's harbor with the party of Paul's friends and clients. That same closed, resentful look she had noticed that night was evident this evening. He had the triumph of a new job now behind him. He was flying again, which was what he loved and what he knew inside loops and out. Something else must be bothering him. "Hey," she said with a smile, touching him on the sleeve. "I'm sorry I've been so busy this evening, but I've missed you. Did you miss me?"

He shook his head and answered sullenly. "You have enough wine to keep me occupied." Some of it sloshed over the rim of the glass from hasty pouring. "Sorry," he apologized. "I'll clean that up. At least that's something I know how to do."

She looked at the others in the living area. "It's just a party, Marcus," Tara said softly. She picked up some napkins from the buffet table and mopped up the spilled wine.

"Wrong," he muttered, glaring at her over the rim of the wineglass. She remembered his angry eyes from that earlier meeting. His eyes had always given away the inner secrets of his soul. Now, behind the anger, she saw frustration and pain and knew that he wasn't just mad because she had left him alone for a while at the party. His anger went deeper. "It's not *just* a party. It's the whole thing that separates you from me. Intelligence." He said the word as if he expected her to wash out his mouth with soap afterward but didn't care for the punishment as a consequence. "This is your crowd, not mine."

"Oh, Marcus," she said, trying to offer comfort by taking his hand. "Not now." She wished the party would go away so that only she and Marcus would be left. She didn't want to watch the hurt in his eyes and feel helpless to do anything to ease his pain. But she couldn't very well get into an in-depth conversation with a roomful of interruptions. He deserved better. He needed a wealth of tenderness and understanding in order to break through the barriers he was building between them with the bricks and mortar of her education and his lack of schooling.

"No," he said, "not now. At least give me credit for a little bit of smarts. I'm not going to make a big scene in front of all of your friends."

"That's not what I meant," she said, anger spicing her words. "I *do* give you credit for intelligence. A lot of it. You're the one who's so hard on yourself. All I meant was I'm not prepared to deal with this right now. In order to work through this, we need a quiet, relaxed atmosphere."

"And a couch," he added, "with a little diploma on the wall—" He turned and pantomimed a plaque hanging there. "To sanctify the patient-therapist relationship. Don't practice your doctor's degree on me, Tara. You haven't fully earned it yet."

Her jaw popped open. She watched him finish another glass of wine. She couldn't remember seeing him drink this much, ever. During the summer he had been flying and hadn't been allowed to drink. The weekend they had spent together in Texas, there had been wine with meals but very little in between. She told herself it was the alcohol making him irrational and adding to his irritability. She wouldn't make much progress trying to reason with him in this state. "I'm sorry," she said. "I certainly didn't mean to sound like I was looking down on you. I care about you, Marcus. I'd like to get to the bottom of what's bothering you. And okay, yes, I am studying to be a psychologist. I have had some practice in counseling, so I might just have some ideas on how we can work this out because of the *training* I've had." She took a breath and hoped he had caught her emphasis on the word. She didn't want to call her knowledge education, since education in his eyes was a dirty word. "I never meant to imply that you were a mental case."

Guests started milling into the dining area, returning to the buffet table. Marcus smiled politely and Tara matched him smile for smile. They stood there, tensely smiling at one another like duelists in a gunfight, each waiting for the other to make the first move or fire the first angry shout. And that's how Julie found them when she arrived at the party with her boyfriend.

Distracted, Tara let her eyes drop from Marcus's intense gaze. It had always been that way and probably always would. He could outstare her no matter how hard she tried to hold his gaze.

"So you're the dreamboat Tara's had her head in the clouds about since she got back this summer," Julie said, once Tara had introduced her roommate. "And I guess you met Dick?" She looked around the room to see him trying to be the life of the party while everyone did their best to ignore him. "Tara really outwitted him with that hitchhiking scheme of hers. She really knocked the socks and hiking boots off him." Julie looked from one to the other, sensing the tension but uncertain which one of them it stemmed from. "But of course the hitchhiking wouldn't have been a success without you." Flattery was getting her nowhere with Marcus. "Well, this is a surprise, meeting you like this. Tara didn't tell me you were coming, you sly fox, you." She playfully hugged her roommate, looking for a quick escape.

"It was a surprise to me, too," Tara said.

"But the surprise was really on me," Marcus commented.

Julie felt as if she were a net in a tennis match. Everything was flying over her head. Marcus was getting angry, but she wasn't sure why. Had he taken an instant dislike to her? "Well, it's such a surprise to have you at the party," she said lamely to Marcus, then moved behind his shoulder. She made a face at Tara that said, *Good luck speaking to the Sphinx*.

Tara was trying to decide how best to handle Marcus. Take him for a walk around the block to sober him up? Seduce him to sense in the bedroom? Or just abduct him and worry about what would happen later?

"There you are, you two," Della said, coming between Marcus and Tara. "I've watched you two making eyes at each other all night."

"That was **not**hing compared to now," Tara said, trying to make light of the antagonism building like thunderclouds between them. The air was tenser than it had been in the alleyway in Bermuda. The outcome didn't look as if it would be half as pleasant.

"I think it's highly romantic the way you two met," Della said, oblivious to their argument. "Watching you tonight, it's like you have a secret reason for celebrating."

"We did," Marcus muttered. The news of his job had seemed ages ago. They hadn't even begun to talk about it as he had pictured doing all week. There had been so little time before the guests began arriving.

Marcus was a man who felt things deeply. But somewhere between the feelings and the expression he got lost. Tara had to make him see that she couldn't read his mind to understand where all of the hurt was coming from. No matter what he might have thought in accusing her of playing psychologist with him, she would never be much of a therapist if she ignored the needs and pain of the man she loved.

"What is it?" Della insisted. "Are you two secretly engaged or something?" She looked from Marcus to Tara; then her eyes settled on Marcus.

His voice was clipped as he replied, "Ask Tara. She's the one who knows all the answers." Then he set down his glass, none too steadily, and walked out.

Chapter Thirteen

"Did I say something wrong?" Della asked, staring after Marcus.

"No," Tara replied, her exasperation for Marcus, not Della. "But he took it that way. It's not your fault. Not anyone's really; just something he has to work out."

"I'm so sorry. I shouldn't have tried to be so cute, but the two of you looked so special together, and I guess I was feeling my age." She smiled at her own joke.

"It's okay," Tara reassured her. "I think he's taken the whole party the wrong way, not just what you said. He has a lot on his mind. Don't worry." The last, she said for herself. "Excuse me, Della, but I think I'd better find him."

Julie had just poured her first glass of wine and was heading for the buffet table when Tara collared her and explained, "Since I was here so early, it's all your party now. I hate to leave you with everything, but I have to go after Marcus."

"What? Why?" She looked around, noticing his absence. "Where is he?"

"I hope just in the driveway, getting some fresh air," Tara said, trying not to let the alarm creep into her voice. "I don't like to think he's trying to drive after all he's been drinking." She tried to count the number of times she had seen him refilling his glass from the selection of wines at the bar. There was no telling how many times he had gone back when she hadn't noticed.

"What happened?" Julie asked; then, sensing the answer to that would take more than a one-line answer, Julie offered, "Take my car if you need it. It's parked on the street. Yours is impossible to get to."

Tara smiled at her roommate's intuitive concern and reached for the outstretched keys. "Thanks," she said, easing toward the door before anyone could involve her in a long-drawn-out discussion.

It was a perfect fall evening. The air was crisp, filled with the smell of wood smoke. A dog was barking on the next street. Lights from the nearby houses said it was still early. But Tara ignored all of that as she searched the dusky light for Marcus. He couldn't have gotten very far, but she had delayed long enough inside to give him enough of a head start to jump in his car and drive off.

Her heart lodged in her throat as she looked for the silver van and didn't see it looming over the other vehicles. Maybe he had flown into town. She had been so excited to see him, she hadn't asked for details of how he had gotten there. Of course he would have done that, she reasoned. He was a pilot, after all. Flying in would have meant he had taken a taxi to her house or hired a rental car. She had no idea what *that* could look like. Her eyes flew over all of the cars in the driveway and parked on both sides of the street. She recognized some of the students' vehicles. Then the cool night air and her professional calm combined to make her think logically. Marcus had arrived before he had known there was going to be a party. He would have parked in the driveway and found himself blocked in by the other guests unless he had parked on the street in the first place.

She looked at the head of the driveway, and there he sat, in the driver's seat of a small compact, unable to go anywhere unless he plowed a path through the perfectly manicured lawn and flower beds. Thank goodness he was too much a gentleman to play bumper cars in the driveway. Calmly she walked toward the rental car, taking deep breaths as she tried to compose herself and decide how to act and what to say. She had to be careful not to act like a psychologist and upset him further. But she had to get at the bottom of his feelings to understand what upset him most. Maybe Della's implications about a secret engagement had touched off his anger. Maybe he always acted like a temperamental child when he drank too much. She shivered, trying to sort out all of the possibilities.

Sensing her approach, Marcus glanced up and saw her. She couldn't help wondering if he had deliberately waited for her to follow him. He started the engine and tried to back the car in the narrow space. When that didn't work, he tried to move it forward, angling it away from the garage. There was more room in front. If he turned sharply, he could barely slip past the corner of the house without clipping the birdbath. Tara hoped he didn't realize that as she got closer to the driver's side.

Before he realized what she was doing and almost without thinking herself, she opened the door and plucked the key out of the ignition. *Treat it lightly,* she told herself, *at least until you figure out what's at the heart of his aches.* "Hi," she said with a smile as if he had just driven up and she were a car-wash attendant. "Going my way?"

He glared at her. Even in the dusky light from the street and romantic candles lining the walk, his eyes were full of unspoken words, as powerful and direct as the first time their glances had clashed. "I'd like my keys, please." He held out his hand for them.

"What for?"

He stared at her sophisticated black dress as if she were a traffic cop asking for his license. "Listening to the radio," he said sarcastically. "The car doesn't work very well without the keys."

"Keys? What keys?" She tossed them in the air. They landed on the roof with a jangling thud, skidded a few shingles down and lodged there. Tara tried not to think what would be involved in getting them down again—borrowing the neighbor's ladder, and he was the one who always complained about their loud parties.

"What did you do that for?" he snarled, getting out of the car to see where they had landed on the roof. He'd have to be a cat burglar to climb up there. He glared accusingly at Tara. They had been heading for a showdown long before this party. Now that he had worked himself into a good anger, he wanted to make the best of it.

"You shouldn't be driving, Marcus. You don't need the keys. And you couldn't go anywhere, anyway."

"You're treating me like a child."

"You're acting like one."

Another penetrating stare was his answer. He knew that. It was how he felt around her educated friends. They were the same kind of people Paul Redding liked to hang around with. And if she hadn't been one of them, like Paul, he would never have met her in the first place. It might have been better if he hadn't. He wouldn't have come to care so damned much about her in spite of the impossibility of their situation.

Behind his angry eyes, Tara glimpsed confusion and a dazed kind of pain. Whatever had touched off his temper that evening, she guessed it was something he had been struggling with alone for a long time. Shock treatment wouldn't work with him. Love and kindness would, if she could get him to calm down enough to listen and if he would trust her enough to tell her what was bothering him. "I can't read your mind," she said softly, pleading for an understanding of what had hurt him.

"No? You're pretty good at reading everything else. The only use I'd have for some of those highbrow books of yours is to keep a short table leg from wobbling."

Tara sighed. So that was it. He was feeling the lack of his education again. She had thought they had talked through that in Texas when she had visited him. She could have kicked herself for not realizing how much deeper his feelings went on that touchy subject. Bowing like a courtly footman, she invited, "Which would you prefer, to ride or walk?"

"Ride or walk where?"

"I haven't decided yet," she answered. "That's the surprise." She kept her voice light. She hated confrontations and angry shouting. It never solved problems. She shook slightly as she realized there might be a lot of healthy shouting taking place between them before the night was through.

"I'm not going back to that party," he stated.

"I don't recall asking you to." She wondered if someone had said something to him. Dick, perhaps. She wouldn't put it past him. Dick had made the other students think Tara was better than they were. It would be just like him to fill Marcus's head with that nonsense, too.

He took a deep breath and turned away, pounding his fist against the car. Tara hoped he hadn't hit it hard enough to dent the roof, but she did wish he had felt the pain. Something needed to get through his thick senses. Her words seemed to be having little effect. "Look at your friends in there, all those people who talk a different language than I do. How do you ever expect me to fit in with that crowd?"

"I don't," she answered simply. "Not if you don't want to. I'm proud of you; that's why I want you to know everything about me and my world."

"They don't make English-Psychology, Psychology-English dictionaries for people like me to follow the dialogue. We have nothing in common."

"You know, we don't have to make all of my friends *our* friends. I want to know your friends and make new friends together with you." She took his arm, wanting to be closer to him physically if she couldn't reach him any other way. She sensed that he needed her, and she wanted to make him see how much she needed him in her life.

"I just don't fit in with those people in there, talking about cognitive restructuring and sublimate whatevers."

"They would probably feel the same way boarding one of your airplanes when you were the sole authority. The language of flight is just as confusing."

Just when she thought he was softening, she saw that hard look in his eyes again. He moved away from her. "You have all the answers, don't you?"

She shook her head. "If I did, we wouldn't be playing search and seizure in the driveway. Actually," she admitted, glancing up at the roof with her hands on her hips, "I should have hidden the key on my body." She faced Marcus. "Then we could have played search and seizure in the backseat of the car. Of course, lovers' lane would be a more appropriate spot. I wonder where the current lovers' lane is?"

The innuendo wasn't fazing him. It had taken him a long time to build up his anger. He wasn't going to let it go so easily. "Is lover one of your convenient labels, too? Like schizophrenic? I don't think it applies anymore."

"I guess you wouldn't," she agreed. "You're not acting like a lover." She stopped playing games and said softly, "Marcus, what is it going to take to make you realize how much I care about you? I don't want to see you kill yourself in a drunk-driving accident before I have a chance to tell you I love you."

As dark as the night was with the moon behind a cloud, she thought she had never seen his eyes look darker. After one intense moment he looked away. "You got one thing right," he mumbled.

"What's that?"

"I must be drunk to think I heard you say you love me. It just doesn't fit."

"Why not?" Tara argued. "Most men put women they idealize on a pedestal. But you've put me on some kind of educational podium, Marcus. Do you think I'm so high up on this stage you've imagined in your mind that I can't lower myself to be human and fall in love with you?''

Whether it was because of his slow reflexes from the amount of drink he had consumed or the shock of what she was saying, he didn't respond. Tara swept on.

''What gives you the right to think that you're better than me because you've had to work your way up from the bottom? Do you think it's been easy making my way in a field that for years was dominated by men, fighting a man like my ex-husband, who had to dominate me in everything? He was never happy about anything that mattered to me. He never gave me the first ounce of encouragement or support, yet I did everything I could to make him understand that I didn't want to compete with him. But nothing was good enough for him.''

Marcus heard her voice trembling as the pain of her past relationship came tumbling out into the open between them. He wanted to reach out and hold her, end this silly argument, end her pain and his, both of which were rooted in the past. He knew her hurt because he had lived with the same kind of spouse, self-centered, interested only in appearances, never taking the time to listen to what her mate needed, wanted, thought. And now, damn it, he was doing the same thing to Tara, who loved him. He had become self-centered, concentrating on his problems, his inadequacies, when she had done nothing to make him feel any less a man.

''Do you think waving my degrees will give me a free passport to a success you'll never know?'' she demanded. "Because it won't, Marcus. You're only as good as you believe yourself to be. It has nothing to do with how many years you've spent with an open book. It doesn't mean that I'm any better than you. And if you think it does, then maybe we weren't meant for each other. I don't intend to spend my life with someone who thinks I'm the superior officer."

Tara touched his arm and considered it a sign of progress that he didn't try to shake her off. She might be able to convince him their educational differences didn't matter to her, but as long as it was a problem in his mind, it would be a stumbling block to their future. "Marcus, I will not apologize for who I am. I thought that that was what had attracted you to me in the first place."

"We're on two different levels."

She stood on her tiptoes to make herself taller than him. "Sure, as long as you keep looking up your nose at me." His eyes shifted away from her. She paused to catch her breath. "Marcus," she began on a softer tone, "I love you. I thought we were building a relationship of equals, not inventing equations that always balance in my favor. I don't want to be superior. I have to keep up that facade when I'm with clients who are looking to me for guidance. I want to be myself when I'm with the man I love. I want to be able to let down my guard and have my weaknesses and insecurities show instead of feeling as if I always have to act like some superhuman machine."

He looked at her as if he wanted to reach out and touch her, but pride held him back. "I can't believe you say you love me. It can't be that simple. No one has ever loved me so unreservedly before."

She watched him struggle with himself, and then she spoke softly, hoping to tip the balance toward her. "I'm a woman, Marcus, not a book. I have the same needs as you do to be loved."

He took her hand and looked at her. Even in the dim light she could tell that there was a lot of confusion he wanted to sort through. She held his hand, not daring to move closer for fear of having him run away. "Let's go for a walk," she suggested, and led him past the parked cars into the street, along the route she took each morning on her aerobic walk.

"Marcus," she began, "you mean a lot to me. I don't think you realize how much you've changed my life." She thought of her applications for internship. Six months earlier she would have laughed if someone had told her she would be letting a man influence the decision on where she moved. "Before I met you, I was just going through the motions of life, listening to other people's problems, feeling removed because I could solve things by giving them a perspective they couldn't find themselves. But I never let their pain and emotion affect me other than superficially, as a sympathetic ear. I was the perfect cool professional until I met you, Marcus."

He looked at her but still didn't speak.

"For the first time in my life I feel like I have a chance for a real relationship with a man. I've felt your caring, that you've been interested in me for who I am, not what I can be. And I feel very protective of that relationship. Relationships take work. They don't happen all by themselves. When there's a problem, both people need to work on it. Maybe we haven't done this sooner, because I didn't realize how deeply you felt about my schooling. It's not a problem you should have to figure out on your own, Marcus. I love you and want to share everything with you, the bad and the good. But you have to let me help sometimes.''

Tara matched her steps to his and wondered what more she could say. Her speech had already lasted for three blocks. The silence stretched even farther. Tara was feeling chilled and wished she had taken the time to grab a jacket before she had left the house. She thought of the night she had worn Marcus's sweater on the walk in Norway. Would this be the last time they walked together or the beginning of something even better? Ordinarily she would have snuggled closer to Marcus for warmth, but she sensed his fragile vulnerability and didn't want to disturb his thoughts when he needed to digest what she had said. The silence made her feel as if the gulf he imagined between them was becoming wider.

''Are you always so wise, Tara?'' Marcus finally asked.

''Oh, Marcus,'' she said in exasperation, losing what little was left of her professional cool. ''Don't give me impossible standards to live up to. I'm trying to tell you I'm only human.''

''I didn't mean it that way,'' he said, tightening the grip on her hand, which he held, and pulling her close.

''What, then?'' she asked, feeling defensive, reversing roles.

''Are you always so wise to know what I needed and what was behind all of my irrational anger before I even came to terms with it myself?'' He stopped with her and faced her in the moonlight. ''It's not the party that's the problem. It's not you and your education. It's me and how I've felt for years about not finishing high school. It's always bothered me, but not as much as it did when we met.''

"Why? I never meant to make you feel as if my education was more important or better than yours.''

"I know," he said, touching her cheek with the back of his hand. "I did that, and a good job of it, all without your help." He paused, looked away, then forced himself to meet her searching eyes directly. "Meeting you made me face that part of myself I've felt ashamed of all these years.''

Tara put her arms around him. It had taken a great deal of courage for him to admit that not only to himself but to someone else. "Oh, Marcus," she said, tears filling her eyes. "I love you so much.''

"Do you?" he asked, his voice muffled as he buried his face in her hair. "Can you? I'm not the macho male like that Dick Shaw in there or Paul Redding. I can't pretend something like this doesn't matter to me. It matters a hell of a lot to me, but I don't know what to do about it. I can't change either of our pasts, and really wouldn't want to, but—''

"Marcus," she assured him, "it takes a strong man to admit that you can be vulnerable. That's exactly what I've been trying to tell you. I don't always like being the strong, invincible image you keep trying to make me out to be. We can balance each other at times like this. That's what a real relationship is all about, especially when it's built on love.''

He cradled her face between his palms. "When we met this summer, you were like a dream to me. I couldn't believe that you could be interested in me. Even when Paul turned up in D.C. without you, I didn't want to admit how much you'd come to mean to me.'' He smiled wryly, distracted momentarily by the lights of a passing car. "But I guess it was pretty obvious to everyone else when I decked him."

Tara laughed nervously. This was what she had waited to hear, that Marcus cared as much about her as she did him. The problem of their educational backgrounds would still need a great deal of understanding and patience until it was worked out for Marcus's sake, but this evening marked the beginning of their knowing one another on a deeper level. "And I didn't even have a chance to tell you goodbye. I was so angry with Paul, because I thought I'd never see you again. I kept telling myself you were smart enough to take care of yourself."

"But you were worried about me," she interrupted him. "You knew I was vulnerable, that I had needed you for the previous two weeks." He nodded. "I still need you, Marcus," she whispered. "You've brought me something very precious that no man has ever done for me before."

"You know I can't afford expensive presents for you now. What could I have given you?"

"You bared your soul to me, Marcus. You showed me where you hurt."

He folded her into his arms, and she felt him trembling as he realized how close he had come to losing her because of his own foolish pride. Very softly he began to tell her, "When you love someone, you don't try to change them. I've always known that was how it should be, but—" He was silent a moment, and Tara could tell he was having difficulty controlling his emotions, putting his fragile feelings into words. "But no one has ever accepted me as I am until now. I had to quit school because the job I was working after school wasn't paying enough to give my wife the things she felt she couldn't live without. I had to work an extra job on the side just to get enough money to finish my flight training. It might have taken me a lot longer than it did to earn my pilot's license if an old barnstorming pilot hadn't felt pity for me and taken me up every chance he had.''

"Oh, Marcus," Tara said, hugging him tighter, stroking his back as if to tell him that he had finally come home. "Didn't she understand what that meant to you?"

"We were both young. You only think for yourself at that age. At least that's what she taught me and why it's taken me so long to learn otherwise." He paused again, kissing her on the temple and smoothing her hair with both hands as if he had just arrived in the Orient and found the most precious of gifts to take home. "All my life I've made decisions that put my needs last. They were my decisions, clearly made, and I can't say that I regret them now or had any other choice; but the choices never allowed me to do what I really wanted."

Tara kept stroking him, knowing that he had probably never shared this information with anyone. Before they could move forward together, he had to put the past behind him.

"Before marriage, there was my mother. She had four kids to support, and I was the oldest. So I went to work in the corner drugstore when I was twelve, pushing a broom, but it was work. Back then, every little bit helped. Even after I was married, I sent what I could home, until my little brothers got out of school and were on their own. I guess that's partly why I got married in the first place."

"Why?"

"To get out of the house, to feel as if I were on my own instead of the provider for a family of five. But it didn't work that way. I found myself in a better-built prison than before, and there was no love to make the effort worthwhile."

Tara looked at him and smiled. "You're on your own now and making your own decisions. You were the one, after all, who decided to go back to school."

He nodded. "I know, and I'm glad I'm getting my diploma. But it still seems so ridiculous to be studying American history stacked up against the books you're memorizing."

"I would be equally intimidated sitting in the pilot's seat of your plane. And think of the responsibility resting on your shoulders, Marcus, the lives of everyone in that aircraft. It makes what I'm doing look like mud pies."

He shook his head, respecting her more for the loving care she had shown him that evening. Resting his forehead against hers, he said, "I don't want to be alone anymore, Tara. I don't want to always feel as if I'm grounded, watching the important things in life fly past me. You're important to me. That's part of what I came here to tell you this weekend. I want to spend more time with you, get to know you better. I want to figure out a way that we can both live in the same city. I want to marry you. I love you so much."

"Oh, Marcus," she said, throwing her arms around his neck and pressing tightly against him, oblivious of the car that drove past, raking them with its headlights. His lips were cool against hers, but the flame of their passion soon warmed them, filling her with a yearning excitement to be much closer. "Of all the documents that will one day be framed on the walls of my office, there won't be any more important to me than our marriage certificate. I love you.''

He buried his face in her hair, stroking her back as if he couldn't believe he held this precious dream in his arms. "Am I to take that as a yes?" he mumbled, too filled with emotion to say much more, feeling too vulnerable to assume her actions confirmed the message his heart wanted to know.

"Yes, my love. Do you think I'd waste a perfectly good proposal like that?"

"It could have been done more romantically," he said, and they both remembered the steamy afternoon in Bermuda when he had held back from kissing her because he wanted the first time to be memorable.

"You're romantic," she said joyously. "You make everything else romantic." As she threw back her head, smiling at him, the moon came out from behind a cloud and lit her face.

Marcus put his hands on her cheeks to raise her face and smiled at this woman who loved him. She would always be a cross between serious professional and impish minx. It was part of what he had fallen in love with. "I didn't plan on asking you to marry me tonight, or even this weekend."

"Why not?"

"It's too soon. I wanted to give you more time to get to know me and what you're letting yourself in for."

"I won't change my mind, Marcus Landry," she told him in no uncertain terms.

"I'm counting on that," he said with a smile.

"Why did Della's remarks make you angry?"

"It wasn't Della. It was the party. Before I came here, marrying you was all I thought of after your visit to Texas. But when I saw all of your cultured friends, it just seemed like the impossible dream. I'm still not certain this is really happening. I suppose we should go back to the party and really give them something to talk about."

"I'd like to," Tara admitted, "but are you sure?"

"When you make a crash landing, you go up again as soon as you can. I should start adjusting to the friends we're going to meet from your world, shouldn't I?" He shook his head, kissing her cheek. "I was a heel to walk out on you like that. It's not my style to run from a fight, but I just couldn't handle it tonight."

"It's okay," she said with an impish grin. "If you hadn't, I might have had to wait weeks or months to hear you say you love me and want to marry me. Personally, I enjoyed the time alone." She hugged him again, feeling as if she would never get enough of looking at him and loving him. "Tell me again, Marcus. I'm not sure I believe it, either."

"I love you," he said, speaking from the heart. "And I'd like to remove the guests from your room right now—" he ran his hands down the length of her back, remembering the silky feel of her skin as she had lain with him that afternoon "—so that we could have the bed to ourselves. I suddenly feel as if one might come in handy right now."

"You, too? I thought I was the only one feeling weak in the knees." As she looked again at the mischievous light in Marcus's eyes, she knew that it was the way he would make her feel for a long time to come. "Maybe we should elope."

"That's not a bad idea, but I want to do it right for you, right down to the last detail. And we'll invite all of our friends, *yours* and mine."

"It sounds romantic, just like you," she said, hugging him again. "But the only reason I suggested it is because I can just imagine the kind of postcard I want to send Julie."

"And what would it say?"

"'Dear Julie. When Marcus and I walked out of the party, I never realized what a hike it would lead to. We're getting hitched! With love from our honeymoon.'" She faced him. "And I'd sign it 'Tara *and* Marcus.'"

Three months later, when Tara accepted her internship in Houston and Marcus received his high school diploma, Tara mailed the postcard.

Harlequin American Romance

COMING NEXT MONTH

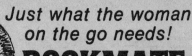
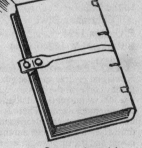